# THE SECRETS AND SCANDALS OF MELODY MOSS

*To Jenny and Jim,*
*who not only gave me life,*
*but also a love of books.*

PENGUIN BOOKS

UK | USA | Canada | Ireland | Australia
India | New Zealand | South Africa | China

Penguin Random House Australia

Penguin Random House Australia is part of the Penguin Random House group of companies whose addresses can be found at global.penguinrandomhouse.com.

First published by Penguin, an imprint of Penguin Random House Australia Pty Ltd, in 2026



Cover and internal design by Caroline Lee © Penguin Random House Australia Pty Ltd

Printed and bound in Australia by Griffin Press, an accredited
ISO AS/NZS 14001 Environmental Management Systems printer

NATIONAL LIBRARY OF AUSTRALIA

A catalogue record for this book is available from the National Library of Australia

MIX
Paper | Supporting responsible forestry
FSC www.fsc.org FSC® C018684

ISBN 9 781 76135 419 9 (Paperback)

We at Penguin Random House Australia acknowledge that Aboriginal and Torres Strait Islander peoples are the Traditional Custodians and the first storytellers of the lands on which we live and work. We honour Aboriginal and Torres Strait Islander peoples' continuous connection to Country, waters, skies and communities. We celebrate Aboriginal and Torres Strait Islander stories, traditions and living cultures; and we pay our respects to Elders past and present.

# THE SECRETS AND SCANDALS OF MELODY MOSS

Helen Dallimore

PENGUIN BOOKS

# CHAPTER 1:
# Year 7, Term 2 – Let's Go!

Sunday, 27 April
7.04pm

Mum said when I turn thirteen, I'll start to feel different.

**Like,**

**different *how*?**

I'm not a fan of change. I'm perfectly fine as I am, thank you.

I know, I know – there's the whole 'butterfly out of a cocoon' thing, **blah blah blah**. But what about all those changes that **don't** work out so great?

Like:

- The painful, inevitable rise of a zit.
- Bad plastic surgery.
- Demonic possession.
- Leaving last term's sandwich in your lunchbox all holidays, which is certainly, absolutely, not-at-all what happened to me.

Mum also said that soon I'll have a 'growth spurt'. Sounds gross, right? Anything that spurts is a no from me.

Tomorrow is the first day of Term Two. Last term I didn't know what to expect, which is lucky because if I *had* known what was to come, I would have been even more nervous, because Term One was **intense**, to say the least.

In short:

- I got unceremoniously dumped by my best friend from primary school, Abby, on day one.
- I made friends with Victor, an actual boy – a species previously thought to be Smelly, Dumb, Gross and Of No Useful Purpose.
- I survived my first ever life-threatening crush on Tyler, who ended up going out with my ex-best-friend Abby. Yes, it was as bad as it sounds.
- I went from being a Total Social Outcast with unfashionable hair, to being the successful co-writer of the smash-hit Year 7 musical, along with my new best friend, Victor.
- My biggest secret – something I thought only happened to me – happened to Victor, too . . .

You see, Victor and I share a common bond. We are both obsessed with musical theatre. Since I was little, musical-theatre characters, who I thought were totally made up in my head, have visited me when I'm feeling down or need advice. I presumed it was just a *Me Thing*, but on the last day of term when Victor was at my place after school, **he saw one of them too**.

An old-fashioned revolutionary soldier, who tried to steal Victor's pizza.

We haven't really had a chance to talk about it since. Victor is a bit of a quiet one, plus he went to music camp for the holidays. I went to Byron Bay with my dad and my big sister, Ash – who may or may not be human and who said a total of five words to me the entire holiday.

So, tomorrow is the first time I'll have seen Victor since then. We have serious business to discuss!

I'm only just starting to get the hang of the whole high school thing. Surely that's enough change for now. I've got quite good at being twelve – can't I stay here for a while?

Do I have to turn thirteen?

Is it **absolutely necessary**? ***shakes fist at sky***

BTW, I turn thirteen in –

# THREE WEEKS.

*gulp*

Anyway, after Abby dumped me, she started hanging out with The Clones – Enid and Epiphany. They all looked the same, had the same swishy blonde hairdos, spoke the same and acted the same – basically they were one person split into three. But after The Ponytail Incident, when my hair got chopped off (long story – well, **short** story now LOL), I got a fabulous short haircut and by the end of last term they were all copying **me**!

So, at least one thing I don't have to be worried about tomorrow is my hair.

I'll also be wearing a **New Bra**. My first bra managed to tangle, strangle and publicly humiliate me last term, but I'm a Bra Expert now.

I fear no bra.

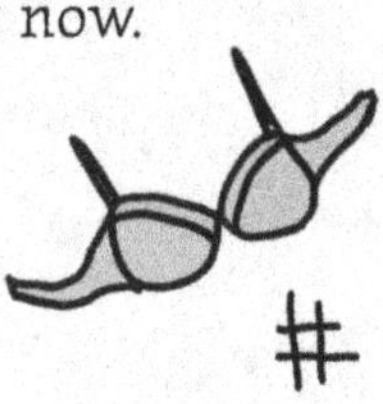

I have Fab Hair, Bra Confidence and I'm ready to nail Term Two.

What could possibly go wrong? ☺

# CHAPTER 2: Queen of The Clones

Monday, 28 April
4.53pm

As I sashayed through the school gates this morning, with my fabulous and funky 'pixie cut'* hairdo, I couldn't believe the difference in how I felt compared to last term. The first thing I noticed was that quite a few girls had haircuts just like mine!

***I'm a trendsetter!***

A couple of people smiled and said, 'Hi Melody!'

*People know me now.*

*Google 'pixie cut' for accurate depiction of my fabulousness.

Sure, I *was* briefly famous for talking to myself and having an unverified paper allergy, but after the success of our Year 7 musical last term – a musical I conceived, wrote and directed **thank you very much*** – I like to think I've earned a bit of respect around here.

If only Victor was in my class – I was dying to see him! As I scanned the hallway for him after first period, I bumped into Abby. She was still rocking 'The Melody' haircut, named after me.

*Okay, not completely by myself, my bestie Victor may have contributed, say 50% of the creative input, but still.

***flex***

She'd got taller over the holidays and looked even more grown up.

**Why am I the only girl in Year 7 who still looks like everybody's little brother in a skirt?**

'Hi Melody!' said Abby excitedly.

There was a time when I would've given anything for Abby to be so friendly to me. But after she was so mean last term, I was on my guard.

'Hi Abby.' I smiled back.

'How was Byron Bay?'

'Good, thanks. Hot.'

'Yeah,' she said knowingly. 'When we went there last year, it was super-hot, but I got really tanned!'

*Of course she did.*

She glanced at my legs, which are roughly the shade of hospital sheets, then looked slightly panicked and quickly said, 'But tanning is *so* bad for you! You're smart to stay out of the sun.'

I didn't remind her that I only come in two colours, red and white. Any attempt I make to get a tan only results in a fluorescent cooked-prawn colour, which eventually sheds, snake-like, back to hospital white.

'Yeah. That's me – sun safe,' I said, backing the hell out of there.

'See you at lunch!' she called as she disappeared into the blue-and-white sea of backpacks.

*Oh, that's right!*

The grassy sanctuary that Victor and I found behind the Science Building last term had been invaded by Abby and The Clones. They would probably be there today, all up in our grill, including my ex-crush, Tyler, who is now Abby's boyfriend.

***Blagh!***

I was right. When the lunch bell rang, I ran to our spot as fast as I could to catch up with Victor before the others arrived. But they were already there. Abby, Enid and Epiphany. The Clones. All with my exact haircut.

Last term, Enid secretly recorded me 'talking to myself' in the girls' toilets and sent it to *everyone.* I was the laughing stock of the school for a hot minute, but eventually Enid apologised and I forgave her, so we're all good now.

Maybe this term is going to be about giving people second chances.

*I can be like a benevolent queen.*

*Melody Moss, Queen of The Clones. LOL.*

They were all sitting in a circle with Tyler, who is actually a very nice person. He starred in our musical last year opposite Abby. Abby is a really good singer and actor. Tyler . . . not so much. *awks*

'Hi Melody!' said Abby. 'Move over, Enid!'

Enid looked a bit put-out and shifted about four millimetres to the left.

'Hi guys!' I said, flopping down between Enid and Abby.

'Hi Melody!' said Tyler, flashing his ridiculously perfect smile.

Did I mention that he is jaw-droppingly handsome?

Yeah. **That.**

'Hi Tyler.' I smiled back but averted my eyes. Even though he is Abby's boyfriend now, and no longer my crush, he is still hard to look at.

As I opened my lunchbox, which contained some sort of funky noodle salad (my mum likes 'experimenting with flavour'), I had to admit to feeling kind of cool.

This time last term I was sitting here all alone, resigned to the lifelong destiny of a Social Outcast.

Now, I am officially in a 'friendship group'.

As I was picking the edible flowers out of my salad, I looked up and saw Victor coming around the corner very cautiously, as though approaching a group of potentially angry swans*. You know those ones that chase you?

*Google 'angry swan' and you'll see what I mean. #scary

'Hi Victor!' I said, making room for him next to me and trying to contain my excitement. Victor is a shy person. Not a fan of small talk. Or being in groups. He's more of a one-on-one guy – although, after our musical was such a hit, he has definitely come out of his shell a bit.

A *bit.*

'Hey bro,' Tyler said warmly.

'Hello,' Victor replied, making eye contact with precisely no-one as he sat down next to me on the grass.

'How was music camp?' I asked.

'Oh yes, how *was* it, Victor?' asked Abby, a bit too enthusiastically.

'Good.' Victor is a man of few words.

'Is it for singers as well?' continued Abby. 'Because

since my **huge** success in the musical last term I've been thinking **a lot** about my future and I've decided to focus on performing. Music camp could be really good for me. What do you think?'

Victor looked utterly lost for words and just stared at Abby through his huge glasses.

*I need to rescue him.*

'Maybe you could ask Miss Elliot?' I said, deflecting.

Our music teacher Miss Elliot, BTW, is my favourite. She's kind and lovely and basically saved me last term.

'Good idea, Melody!' said Abby. 'Miss Elliot is *so* nice, isn't she? I really feel like she and I have a special bond.'

Now, I'm not usually the jealous type, but something about the way she said that really made my blood boil and before I could stop myself, I said, 'Yes, I think she's one of those teachers who's especially nice to the kids they feel a bit sorry for. **So** kind.'

I caught Victor's eyes, which went wide at that moment and we both had to look away to stop us cracking up.

Abby didn't seem to notice my dig and went on.

'I wish there was going to be a musical this term. I'm going to miss it **so much**. School is going to be **so boring** now, don't you guys think?'

Enid and Epiphany looked a bit awkward. Neither of them had been involved with the musical and I think they felt a bit left out.

Tyler shrugged and said, 'It was fun, but it's not really my thing. I'm busy enough with school and Billy.'*

*Billy is Tyler's little brother, who I babysat a few times last term.

Billy:

- locked me up,
- ran away from me,
- cut off my hair,
- generally made my life a living hell.

He is five.

'Come on, Melody, Victor! *You* guys will miss it! You wrote it!' Abby said, giving Victor a nudge that nearly toppled him over.

'I'm pretty busy with piano.'

Victor is a brilliant pianist. He might even be a professional one day.

All eyes looked to me. I didn't really want to admit how much I'd miss doing the musical. Even to myself.

'Yes, it was fun, but I'm happy just to focus on school for this term.'

*Sounded convincing.*

'But musicals are your **thing**, Melody!'

*Shut up, Abby.*

'I know.' I shrugged, chewing on a bit of pickled zucchini. 'But maybe it's time to try out some new things. There's more to life than musicals.'

***I can't believe I actually just said that.***

# CHAPTER 3: The Face

Tuesday, 29 April
7.18am

Victor and I are going to catch the bus together after school today. This is a big step for him – normally he gets picked up by his mum. He gets uncomfortable around **Other People** and a bus full of teenagers can be a lot, even if you are one.

5.32pm

Knowing I was going to see Victor was the only thing that got me through my last class, which was Geography.

*snore*

I can't see a future where being able to read a topographic map will be necessary, but let's hope it isn't, because I spent the entire lesson wondering if boring Mr Splitz had an Exciting Secret Life. I was picturing him dancing in a gold sequined bikini and shaking a tambourine, when the bell finally rang and we all got out of there so fast Mr Splitz turned around to see nothing but our dust.

Last term, I discovered a shortcut to the front gate through the basketball court.

Which was usually empty.

But not today.

No. Today, there was a bunch of kids playing basketball in it.

## How rude!

But I'd come this far, and I didn't want to keep Victor waiting, so I decided to stealth around the inside edge, undetectable to the naked eye.

Now, to say that I'm not sporty would be an understatement. I've just never seen the fun in it. All that effort for so little entertainment. I'd much prefer to watch some world-class tap-dancing. I suppose the fact that I've never been very good at sport doesn't help.

My sports CV:

- As fast as a slug.
- Lacks all coordination.
- Has never caught anything, ever.

This meant I was always picked last for team sports in primary school, and there's nothing like rejection to turn you off something for life.

So, I knew entering the basketball court was a risk.

It was **Hostile Territory**.

I took a deep breath, hugged the fence, kept my head down and made no eye contact with The Enemy. I was nearly at the other side, feeling very relieved, when, out of nowhere, something hit me so hard that the next thing I knew I was flat on my back. Well, not completely flat because I was wearing my backpack, so I was:

- flailing like a turtle,
- my limbs not quite on the ground,
- slightly winded,
- gasping silently, my eyes searching for understanding as to what had happened.

I could hear a commotion, voices saying:

*'Oh no! Should we get a teacher?'*

*'I didn't see her – she came out of nowhere!'*

*'Is she all right?'*

*'Are you all right?'*

Then a face hovered into view above me.

An **extremely pleasing** face.

For a minute I thought I might have hit my head and was hallucinating because The Face was *so* pleasing it couldn't have been real.

'Are you okay?' asked The Face. 'I'm so sorry, I didn't see you behind me – I must've bumped into you!'

*Can't talk . . . gasping for air . . .*

'Here,' said The Face, 'let me help you sit up – can you sit?'

Then the arm belonging to The Face slipped around my shoulders and scooped me up like I was a feather.

From my new seated position, I could see that **The Basketball People** had all stopped playing. One of them – the owner of The Face – was crouching next to me. The others were standing around, looking concerned.

'Do you want us to get a teacher?' asked The Face.

***<u>This is beyond mortifying</u>.***

'No, that's okay, I'm fine,' I said, trying to stand up, which is not easy to do while wearing a heavy backpack, as I'm sure you know.

'Here,' said The Face, and he lifted my bag up and me with it, like I was nothing but a strand of hair. As I got up, I realised that The Face belonged to some kind of giant. This kid must have been six foot tall!

'Aren't you Melody Moss?' asked one of the girl players. Her face was very familiar. 'I'm Rebecca, Enid's sister.'

'Oh, hi,' I said feebly. 'I'm sorry, I shouldn't have been in here.'

'That's okay,' said The Face. 'We shouldn't still be here either. They'll kick us out soon. I'm so sorry I knocked you over. I'm Connor. Are you sure you're okay?'

He was so kind and gentle – and, well, tall – that I nearly burst into tears in that way you do when you've had a bit of a shock and someone is nice to you.

***Keep it together, Melody!***

Then I heard a familiar voice call, 'Melody! You all right?'

It was Victor, standing near the exit, looking concerned – but not enough to enter a sports environment where to him, the floor was also lava.

'Coming!' I called, trying to summon some dignity.

'Oh good, is that your boyfriend coming to the rescue?' smiled Connor kindly.

'NO!' I shouted at him. 'I mean, *no*. He's just a friend. Not just *a* friend, my *best* friend, actually, but . . .'

*You're babbling, Melody. Get out of here!*

'Anyway, gotta go, nice to meet you, Connor. See you guys later.'

And I scurried over to Victor and muttered, 'Quick, let's **go**!'

I took off at a clip to put as much distance as possible between me and my humiliation.

'What was all that about?' asked Victor, struggling to keep up.

'Nothing. I just had a bit of a . . .'

What *had* actually just happened? The whole thing was a blur.

'Melody moment?' he suggested with a wry smile.

'Something like that. Can you please stop smiling!'

But apparently he couldn't. At least my embarrassment distracted Victor from the anxiety of being on public transport.

That's me – a walking, falling Public Service.

**Sheesh!**

Now I am home on my bed with my little dog, Toto (who may or may not have a slight flatulence problem), trying not to replay the whole horrific incident on a loop in my mind . . .

. . . and totally failing.

# CHAPTER 4: Do You Hear the People Sing?

Wednesday, 30 April
6.30am

Victor is coming over to watch YouTube after school today. This is the only thing getting me through, after yesterday afternoon's humiliating basketball court incident.

No shortcuts for me today!

*cringe*

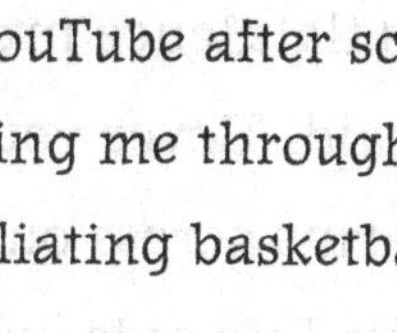

## 7.14pm

It happened again.

The thing.

When Victor and I got home from school, Toto was beside herself at the door, as though I had been gone for ten years and she'd almost given up on ever seeing me again.

Toto's flatulence problem gets worse with excitement, so I said, 'Cover your face!' to Victor and we both put our arms across our faces at the same time as trying to give Toto pats, which was quite the Physical Challenge.

Mum made us afternoon tea with her usual flourish for flavour. She's obsessed with fancy cooking and likes to take it out on the rest of us **LOL**. She's actually a pretty cool mum. A Snappy Dresser, with jet-black hair like my sister. I've got boring brown hair like my dad but we make up for it in personality.

Victor and I sat down in the kitchen to a 'Deconstructed Banana Split with Chocolate Soil', which was a lot, but actually delicious. While she had us captive, Mum took the opportunity to grill us for information. You know what parents are like.

'So, Victor, how was music camp?'

'Good,' Victor mumbled, his glasses fogging up through a mouthful of Caramel Foam.

'And how were your first days, guys? Anything exciting to report?'

'Not really,' I said.

I mean, what did parents **think** happened at school?

'Is Miss Elliot planning another musical this term?' she asked.

'Don't think so. Haven't seen her yet.'

'Goodness, what will you *do* with yourselves?' she joked. 'You might have to focus on actual schoolwork for a change!' Mum found this a *bit* too hilarious.

'I actually have a big piano exam to practise for,' said Victor, with importance.

'And *I* have decided to explore interests other than musicals,' I added, trying to match Victor's seriousness.

This made Mum laugh even harder, which made us both feel slightly indignant.

'Come on, Victor,' I said, taking our bowls to the sink. 'Let's go and see who sings "Defying Gravity"* better.' And I marched off to my room with my head held high, Victor and Toto following behind.

*FYI 'Defying Gravity' is my favourite song from my favourite musical, *Wicked*, which you've probably heard of unless you've just landed here from another planet, in which case – we welcome you.

I have a big computer monitor in my bedroom so I can watch clips and movies from my bed for Maximum Cosiness. Victor and I set ourselves up with cushions and googled 'Who sang "Defying Gravity" better?'*

*Warning: Googling this will take you down a wormhole from which you may never return.

Before I pressed play, I turned to Victor with my most serious face. We still had Unfinished Business to talk about, i.e. the revolutionary soldier we had both seen in this very room at the end of last term.

'What?' he said, looking uncomfortable. Victor is not big on direct eye contact.

'You *know* what,' I answered. 'We haven't talked about what happened!'

'You mean the soldier?'

*'Of course I mean the soldier!'*

'Yeah,' he said, nodding. 'That was weird.'

'That sort of thing happens to me **all the time**, Victor. I tried to tell you.'

Victor shrugged. 'To be honest, I thought he was a friend of yours. I thought maybe you were tricking me.'

'That would be a pretty elaborate trick, to get a grown-up dressed as an eighteenth-century soldier to break in through my window and steal your pizza, Victor.'

'Yeah, I did think that, but I couldn't come up with any other explanation. Except maybe we had, like, a shared hallucination.' He was being annoyingly dismissive. 'It *was* the end of term.'

'What does that have to do with anything?' I was getting exasperated now.

'So, we were really tired.'

'He took a **bite out of your pizza**, Victor. He *spoke* to us! You don't seem to be very freaked out by that.'

'I don't know what you want me to say, Melody,' he said, looking way too relaxed about the whole thing. 'Yes, it was weird, but that sort of thing has never happened to me before, and I'm sure it won't happen again. It's probably a teenage thing. Our brain chemistry is changing. I've heard all sorts of stuff can happen to kids our age.'

*Why is he being so annoying?*

'Made-up characters don't just come to life,' he said.

Right at that moment, Toto, who was lying on the floor, started making a low, grumbling growl.

Then:

- The lock of my cupboard clicked . . .
- The hinge creaked . . .
- The door swung open, just a few inches . . .
- I looked at Victor . . .
- Victor looked at me . . .

'The breeze.' He shrugged.

'The window's shut,' I whispered, slightly nervous about what or who was to come.

Toto suddenly ran over and jumped into the cupboard, barking furiously.

Then we heard a loud voice from inside say, '*Sacré bleu!* My boot! 'E 'as 'old of my boot!' in a very thick French accent.

Victor dived behind a cushion.

But this wasn't my first rodeo, and I knew there was nothing to be afraid of, so I opened the cupboard and . . .

. . . out fell a French Revolutionary Soldier, with Toto latched onto his knee-high boot.

The soldier quickly leapt to his feet, trying to recover his dignity.

'I 'ear we 'av an unbeliever in ze room!' the man

said, looking fiercely at Victor. 'Is it **YOU**?'

Victor peeked out from behind the cushion, white as a sheet and completely dumbstruck.

*That will teach him not to listen to me.*

'Victor hasn't met anyone like you before, that's all,' I said, trying to be chill about it.

'You mean 'e 'as not met a Frenchman, or 'e 'as not met a **fighter against oppression**?' asked the soldier intensely.

'Well, either,' I replied. 'Mostly, visitors have come to me when I've needed help with something. But we were just about to watch YouTube.'

The soldier looked momentarily confused.

'You do not need my 'elp? You 'ave no problem?'

'Not really. I mean, Victor didn't believe me that characters could come to life, but I think that's sorted now, thank you.'

The soldier looked down his nose at Victor and squinted his eyes.

''Zis boy is ze problem? You want me to dispose of 'im?' said the soldier, standing over Victor, who was becoming smaller by the second.

'NO! No, he believes now, don't you, Victor?'

'Yes,' said Victor feebly, still clinging to the cushion for emotional safety.

'I want you to say it!' goaded the soldier. 'Give me a *Vive la Révolution!*'

'*Vive la Révolution*,' murmured Victor weakly.

The soldier took Victor's security cushion and threw it on the bed.

'I cannot 'ear you! Louder!'

'*Vive la Révolution!*' shouted Victor.

'*Une* more time! Everybody!'

He waved his hands in a gesture for us to stand up.

***'Vive la Révolution!'*** we all shouted at the top of our lungs as we jumped on the bed with our fists in the air. Even Toto gave an enthusiastic bark.

The soldier seemed pleased with that. He **looked** at me.

'You 'ave no more problem?'

'No more problem. Thank you,' I replied.

'Zen, *au revoir*!' he said and started singing what I think was the French national anthem as he marched back into the cupboard.

Victor was clearly in shock. He sat dead still for a few seconds, then got up slowly and went over to the cupboard.

'He's gone,' he said, peering in.

'Yep,' I agreed with a shrug. 'That's what they do. Here one minute, gone the next.'

Suddenly there was a very loud **BASH** on my bedroom door.

'Oh God, what *now*?' said Victor, eyes wide.

Before I could answer, my door swung open and there stood Ash, Queen of the Underworld, Mistress of Darkness, looking furious.

'I am **trying to work** upstairs, Melody, and I cannot do so with all of you shouting at the top of your lungs.'

Then she looked around the room, confused.

'Is it just you two? I'm sure I heard more voices than that. Were you singing in French?'

'Oh, we were watching a clip from *Les Mis**,' I said, thinking fast.

**Les Mis (short for Les Misérables) is a musical about the French Revolution, which sounds like the most boring thing ever, but I promise you it's actually incred and you will sob.*

'Well, **turn it down**!' Ash yelled and slammed the door behind her.

Victor sat back down and exhaled deeply.

'Is it always like this at your house?' he asked.

'Yep, pretty much,' I answered. 'Sorry.'

But I had to admit, it felt pretty good to finally have someone to share my secret with.

# CHAPTER 5: Keeping the Dream Alive

Thursday, 1 May
5.34pm

First up today I had my favourite subject, music, with Miss Elliot. Miss Elliot has lots of curly red hair and wears floral dresses and is Generally Lovely.

It was *so* good to see her again, I had to stop myself from running up and giving her a big hug. Instead, I just grinned at her like a scary clown* for the whole lesson.

*Under no circumstances google 'scary clown' – unless you want to be up all night. I'm serious. Just don't.

*You did it, didn't you? I tried to warn you. #thoughtsandprayers

After we spent the lesson listening to some very intense classical music by Beethoven, which made half the class twitchy, Miss Elliot stood up and said, 'Okay, musical-theatre lovers!'

*That's me! I'm a musical-theatre lover!*

She caught my eye and winked.

'The musical last term was a **huge** success. Congratulations again to Melody and everyone else involved.'

She led a feeble round of applause. The kid next to me was so unenthusiastic he could only manage to clap with one hand, which ended up like more of a wave.

'It was a terrific experience and a great way for some of our Year 7 students to get to know each other better. But now I think we all need to recover, so we won't be doing another one this term.'

A wave of disappointment washed over me, but I took a deep breath and tried not to show it.

*It's okay, Melody, you said you would start exploring other interests, remember? Brave face!*

'However . . .' Miss Elliot continued.

*Wait, what?*

'I have an announcement.'

*Annnnnd? Don't keep me in suspense!*

'For those of us who would like to keep the dream alive, I'm going to start an after-school **musical-theatre** club, open to students from Years 7 to 10. Anyone interested can sign up on this sheet here on the piano at the end of class.'

*OMG! A musical-theatre club!*

*My heart might actually explode!*

I shot my hand up.

'Yes, Melody? I'm sure you'll be keen to join,' Miss Elliot said with a smile.

'Miss Elliot, what sort of things will the club do?'

She smiled at me conspiratorially. Miss Elliot loves musical theatre almost as much as I do.

'Well, I was thinking we could watch musical films, listen to recordings, even see a show that's on in town together. That sort of thing. Sound fun?'

The kid behind me audibly groaned like it was the worst form of torture he could possibly imagine.

But me? Beside myself with excitement.

I practically shredded the carpet on my way to the piano to sign up.

At lunch I ran up to Victor, bursting with the news.

'What happened to exploring other interests outside of musicals?' he asked with a wry smile.

'I'm still going to do that, Victor. It's only a club, it'll be one afternoon a week, max. **Please** say you'll join!'

'Melody, I've got my big piano exam at the end of term, I have to practise every day.'

'But you **love** musicals! Life can't be all piano! Miss Elliot said we're going to go and see a show in town together! Maybe even one of your favourites will be on, like *West Side Story*!'

I started to sing a song from *West Side Story*, with a bit of a dance routine thrown in (it's that kind of show). My attempt at high kicks eventually got a laugh out of Victor, who then started to harmonise until we were both singing and dancing like five-year-olds on a sugar high.

'OMG, what the actual, you guys?'

Abby had just arrived and was laughing and applauding at our spontaneous dance routine. Realising we were making a spectacle of ourselves, we sat down to open our lunch.

'So, what are you so pumped about?' asked Abby.

*Oh no.*

*Abby will want to be in the musical-theatre club.*

It's not that I don't like Abby. It's just that I don't feel I can trust her since she dumped me on day one of last term, after being best friends since we were, like, five. It was pretty brutal, tbh. Even though she apologised and is nice to me now, I can't tell whether she's being real or fake. But there was no avoiding it, so I told her what Miss Elliot had said.

'OMG – WHAT?!' she squealed. 'That is, like, the **best news ever!** Melody, we are going to have so much fun! It'll be just like the old days!'

And she threw her arms around me, which took me by surprise. My arms weren't ready, so they got kind of pinned to my side and I just had to take it, which was totes awks. As I looked over her shoulder all I could see was Victor's face, which looked like someone had done a wee in his lunchbox.

Just then, Enid and Epiphany rocked up together. They're **always** together. They somehow manage to look fashionable in uniform. How do people do that?

It seems to come down to minor things like . . .

- sock length
- amount of shirt tuck
- backpack height

. . . which altogether creates an impression of stylish and cool. Stylish and cool seem completely out of reach for me, so I just stick to functional.

'Hey Melody, are you okay?' asked Enid, looking concerned.

*Weird.*

'Yeah, why?' I answered, perplexed.

'My sister said you fully stacked it on the basketball court.'

Oh, that's right. I had a Flailing Turtle Flashback with all those sporty kids looking down at me. The horror!

'Oh, I wouldn't say **stacked it**,' I said, trying to look casual. 'Someone bumped into me, that's all. No biggie.'

'Well, you *were* flat on your back,' smirked Victor.

I glared at him.

*Traitor.*

'I was fine! Your sister was very nice. They all were.'

'All **who**?' asked Abby, smelling gossip.

*I do not like this line of questioning.*

'The . . . basketball people. They actually weren't supposed to be in there.'

'Oh, they're all mad for basketball,' said Enid. 'It's one of the sport electives in Year 8. Rebecca and her friends play it every second minute.'

'Hang on,' said Tyler, who had arrived by this stage and was sitting next to Abby. 'How can your sister be in Year 8?'

'We're only fourteen months apart. Some people think we're twins,' said Enid proudly.

'You do look heaps alike,' I said.

'Yeah, everyone says that. We like the same things too. We're super close.' She smiled.

*Hmm . . . interesting.*

It made sense to me now why Enid likes to be the same as Epiphany and Abby, have the same haircuts and look the same. She's always had that with her sister. When you're an observer of human nature, like I am, you notice these things. I can't imagine what it would feel like to be close to my sister, Ash. She barely acknowledges I exist. We don't look anything alike and have nothing in common, but she *is* heaps older than me and potentially a droid.

'Anyway, basketball is really fun, you guys. We should play after school sometime,' said Enid.

'No thanks,' said Epiphany, grimacing.

'I've got piano,' said Victor.

'I've got Billy,' said Tyler.

'*We've* got musical-theatre club,' said Abby, winking at me.

I watched Enid's eager face gradually fall and I couldn't help but feel sorry for her.

Before my brain had time to think through my life choices, my mouth said, 'I'll do it, Enid! I suck at sport, but maybe you can teach me.'

Victor nearly choked on his juice box.

'Really?' she said, her eyes lighting up.

'Well, I said I was going to explore interests outside of musicals, didn't I? This is perfect.'

'Cool!' she said. 'Maybe we can join in with Rebecca one afternoon. I'll ask.'

*Oh no! Not all those tall Year 8 kids I totally humiliated myself in front of!*

'Okay, great! Can't wait!' I lied.

***What on earth have I done?***

8.29pm

Dad was just over for dinner. My mum and dad split up when I was a baby but they're, like, best friends now and he lives around the corner, which people think is weird, but I love it ☺.

Mum made Pineapple Surprise, and we were all really surprised because it didn't seem to have any pineapple in it, but it was nice.

'So, how is Term Two shaping up, Lamb Chop?' Dad always calls me food names; I have no idea why.

'Good, yeah.'

Dad's a composer, so he's super interested in my 'musical journey'. He writes the music you hear when you ring a business and they put you on hold. He says it's a dying art form because nobody rings anyone anymore, everything's online.

'Are you guys doing another musical with Miss Elliot?' he asked.

'Not this term, but she *is* starting up a musical-theatre club!'

'Whacko! That sounds like fun! Can dads join?'

'*Dad!*' groaned Ash, who'd been investigating her dinner for Traces of Pineapple.

'What? I could be a very useful member of the musical-theatre club, thank you very much, Ashley.'

Ash rolled her eyes, but Dad's the only one who gets away with calling her by her full name.

'What happened to exploring other interests outside of musical theatre?' asked Mum, winking.

'**Actually**, Mum, I'm going to start playing basketball with Enid this term.'

*Touché, Mother.*

'Basketball!' She couldn't have looked more shocked if I'd told her I was going to unicycle to Perth.

Ash scoffed.

'What's brought this on, Chicken?' asked Dad, as though I had contracted a rare and concerning disease. 'I thought you hated sport.'

He was right, of course, but I was determined to prove my commitment to exploring other interests.

'Hate is a very strong word, Dad. Anyway, I'm trying something new – you should all be happy for me.'

'Of course we are, Pikelet. You'll be awesome!'

Then Dad tried a kind of fist-bump with me, but I was holding my fork and all the Pineapple Surprise dropped off into Toto's very happy little waiting mouth.

Now I'm in my room lying on my *Beauty and the Beast* doona cover, one of my favourites I've had since I was little. I was just looking on my phone to see what classes I have tomorrow when I got a DM.

hi melody

basketball tomorrow?

after school?

enid

*Yikes! I wasn't expecting that to happen so fast.*

*I need time to psychologically prepare!*

But I've made such a big deal to everyone about trying new things, there's no getting out of it now.

I typed back:

OK COOL

IM IN

THX ENID

MELODY

I just realised I don't have the foggiest idea how you even play basketball! Time for some research.

## 9.06pm

So, after a few minutes on The Internet, I have learned the following things about basketball:

- The aim is to get the ball into the baskety thing, hence the name.
- The baskety thing is high up, so it's quite hard to do.
- The player, therefore, needs to get as close to the baskety thing as possible.

i.e. The player needs to be tall.

And one thing I am not, is tall.

I looked over to my goldfish, Spike, who was doing the rounds of his fishbowl.

'Of all the sports I decide to attempt,' I told him, 'it's one that is height dependent!'

Suddenly I heard a very loud throat clear.

'There are no small parts – only small players!' declared a very posh voice from under the bed.

I nearly jumped out of my skin!

Toto hid under the doona.

I looked over the edge, and out rolled a stocky, middle-aged man with a grey beard, in a black turtleneck and black tights!

Not what I was expecting at nine o'clock on a Thursday night.

He sprang to his feet and sang a brief scale to warm up his voice.

**'Me me me me meeee!'**

'Who *are* you?' I asked.

'Who *am* I?' he snapped. 'How rude! **Don't you know who I am?** Urgh! Show business can be so cruel!' he finished theatrically.

'Are you . . . an actor?'

'I am more than just an **actor**, dear! I am a vessel for storytelling, a channel of life force, a conduit of human emotion!'

***What the heck is a conduit?***

'It's just that the characters who usually come to visit me are musical-theatre types. Do you sing too?' I asked.

'Dear girl, I do it all! I **sing**, I dance, I act, I mime, I speak the verse of Shakespeare, I am what is known in "the business" as a Character Actor. Every musical has one. We might not perform the big numbers, but when we have our moment, we make our mark!' He winked so dramatically that I thought he might sprain a face muscle. 'Sometimes we play villains, sometimes we play animals, sometimes we play items of household furniture!'

'What did you mean when you said there are no small parts?' I asked.

'Only small players!'

'Yes – what does that **mean**?'

'I shall tell you,' he said, striking a storytelling pose. 'It means that although your part may be small, your impact is just as important as anyone else's, and you must treat it as such.'

'Riiight. And . . . how does this apply to basketball?'

He didn't seem to notice this question.

'Though she be but little, she is fierce!' he said, his eyes wide, staring at me.

*This guy is off his rocker.*

'Sorry, what?'

'The Bard, dear. Shakespeare! Don't they teach you **anything** at school?'

'We haven't done Shakespeare yet. Can you give me the gist?'

He looked a bit depressed at that, dropped his theatrical stance, sighed and said, 'You can still play basketball, Shorty.'

And with that, he lay on the floor and rolled back under the bed.

Toto poked her head out from under the doona, clearly relieved he was gone.

'Well, I'm not sure that was very helpful, Toto.'

She agreed.

I do feel a little bit better, though. At least I'm not completely unhinged like that guy.

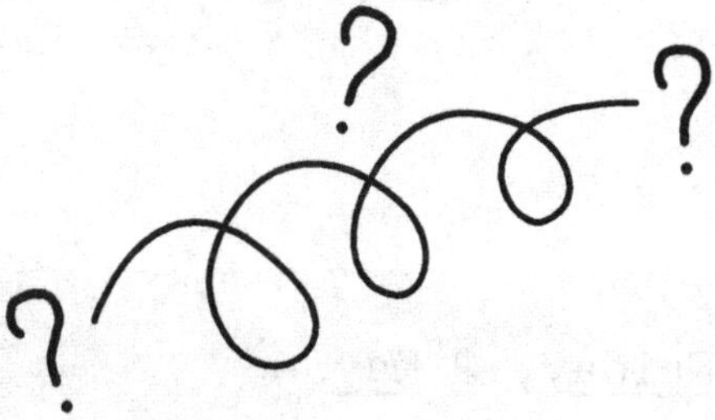

# CHAPTER 6: Dribbling

Friday, 2 May
6.30am

Woke up dreading having to play basketball after school today.

There is so much that can go wrong, such as:

- Complete humiliation in front of cool Year 8 kids.
- My face being smashed in by flying balls.
- Passing out, due to extremely low levels of personal fitness.
- Having to admit to everyone that it was all a terrible mistake.

The only thing getting me through is the thought of our musical-theatre club. I am determined to get Victor to join.

6.30pm

The **Basketball Anxiety** hung over me all day like a huntsman in the shower.

At lunch, I made my way to our usual spot – only to find Abby and Tyler already there.

I could tell by their body language (being an observer of such things), that there was tension between them. Abby was doing the talking; Tyler was looking at the grass.

*Should I interrupt?*

I hesitated a moment too long, and Abby looked up and saw me.

'Melody! Tell Tyler he *has* to join the musical-theatre club! It's going to be *so* much fun!'

Tyler looked slightly pleadingly at me, which put me in a bit of a spot because, tbh, I actually like Tyler more than Abby. He's honest and kind and hasn't totally wrecked my life like she did. But the **Unwritten Girl Code** said I had to support Abby.

'It's definitely going to be awesome but . . . you probably need to look after Billy, don't you, Tyler?' I said, throwing him a lifeline.

'That's right! Yes!' he said, clearly relieved.

'But *we'll* have heaps of fun, Abby!' I said cheerfully.

'But boyfriends and girlfriends are supposed to do things together,' she said miserably.

Tyler suddenly became very interested in a leaf on the ground.

'I heard my parents say it's good for couples to have time apart,' I offered with an encouraging smile.

'Your parents are **divorced**!' she wailed.

'True. Yes. Forgot about that.'

Tyler caught my eye with a bit of a grateful smile and I kind of mock-winced, and for a moment I felt like we were a secret team. (Which I didn't hate.)

Without me noticing, Victor had sat down beside me. He can be **totes stealth**.

'Victor!' said Abby. 'You're joining the musical-theatre club, aren't you?'

*Dang! She beat me to it!*

We all looked at Victor expectantly, but before he could answer, Enid and Epiphany rocked up.

'Melody! All set for basketball?' asked Enid.

'OMG, are you really going to do it?' asked Abby, amused. 'I thought you hated sport.'

'I don't **hate** it, I'm just not very good at it. But all that is going to change!'

*Yep, watch out for Melody Moss: Athlete LOL!*

'Can we come and watch?' asked Abby, a twinkle in her eye.

Abby was enjoying this a bit too much for my liking.

'**NO!**' I shouted, possibly overreacting. 'I mean, maybe later, when I know what I'm doing.'

*Change the subject!*

'Victor.' I turned to him. 'You haven't answered the question. Are you going to join the musical-theatre club?'

Victor paused. All eyes were on him. I probably shouldn't have put him on the spot, but I was desperate.

'Maybe,' he said casually.

'Victor, you are so mysterious!' said Abby.

But I know Victor. He was just avoiding Peer Pressure. I needed to get to him alone.

'You want to come over on the weekend and look up what shows are on in town?' I asked him. 'Then if Miss Elliot asks, we'll know what we want to see.'

'Oh, can I come?' said Abby before Victor could speak. 'That sounds like so much fun!'

***AWKS*** ***Now what do I do?***

Victor was violently staring at me now, but what could I do? If someone invites themselves over to your house, how on earth do you say anything but 'yes' without it being the most awkward awks in the history of awks?

'Of course! The more the merrier!' I lied.

*It will so not be merrier.*

Sometimes I find it hard to believe that Abby and I used to be best friends. But I guess we were both different people back in primary school. Things sure are changing fast. Now I just want to spend time with Victor. It's easy with Victor. He gets me.

'Amazeballs!' said Abby. 'I'll bring lollies!'

'Yay.' I smiled weakly.

Weird silence, during which:

- Enid unfolded and re-folded a chip packet.
- Epiphany became fascinated with her left sock.
- Tyler broke a stick into many smaller sticks.

'You're all welcome to come too,' I said unconvincingly.

Tyler, Enid and Epiphany all quickly mumbled vague excuses. For non musical-theatre nerds, it would've sounded like the worst time ever.

And with Abby there, it probably will be.

The afternoon went by really fast as I hurtled towards The Inevitable. In Food Tech, I forgot to put the honey in my 'healthy muffins', so they tasted like sawdust and sadness. I definitely don't have my mother's flair for cooking.

Once the bell rang, I made my way nervously to the basketball court. On approach, I could see two people there already, throwing balls around and jumping unnecessarily high, in my opinion. They looked like professionals. I felt a bit sick, but I took a deep breath and walked in with as much confidence as I could muster on a Friday afternoon.

'Hi! Melody!'

It was Connor, the tall boy with the **Ridiculously Pleasing Face**.

*Why does he have to be here? It's one thing to fail, but to fail in front of really good-looking people is far, far worse.*

'Enid said you were keen to learn basketball,' he said warmly.

I could barely look at him. Partly because he was so tall, and the sun was behind his head.

'Yes, *so* keen!' I replied. 'But I don't want to interrupt you guys. I've never played before, so I can just watch or . . . whatever,' I said, desperately trying to stall for time.

'We're gonna teach you!' said Enid's sister, Rebecca, walking over to join us. She looks so much like Enid it's spooky.

'Oh, great!' I lied. 'Is Enid here?'

'Behind you!' said Enid, approaching with her bag. It was like seeing double. Enid wasn't as tall as Rebecca, but she wasn't far off. I felt like a hamster next to them all.

'Hi, Enid! Dump your bag and we'll get started,' said Rebecca. 'Once you guys have got the hang of it, maybe you could join our basketball club. We don't have any Year 7s yet!'

*Ha! Not on your life, Beanpole.*

'Okay, let's start with dribbling,' said Connor.

*That cannot be what he said.*

'I'm sorry, what?' I asked.

Connor laughed and sunbeams shot out of his face. Or at least, that's what I saw.

'Not as in drooling!' he said.

They all laughed. I joined in to save face. 'No, **obviously**! Hahaha!'

'It means bouncing the ball. It's how you travel around the court. Like this.'

He started this so-called 'dribbling' and, to be honest, it looked incredibly easy, which was a huge relief. I was slightly mesmerised watching him glide across the court, which he seemed to do in about three strides because his legs are like palm trees.

'Give it a go,' said Connor, handing me the ball. It was heavier and larger than I expected in my small hands. But he made it look so easy, I felt confident I could bounce the thing.

*How difficult can it be?*

I steeled myself and hurled the ball to the ground as hard as I could. The ball then bounced violently back up into my face and sent me flying backwards. I managed to stay vertical, just.

'Are you okay?' asked Connor, looking worried.

'Yep, all good,' I said, although my nose did feel extremely sneezy from the impact. 'I'm guessing that's not how you do it.'

'You only need to bounce it gently,' said Rebecca.

'Yes, right. I suppose that was more spitting than dribbling,' I joked, embarrassed.

'Hahaha! You're funny!' said Connor, cracking up. 'Spitting!'

At least I can make people laugh, which is something.*

'And maybe I should use my hands instead of my face!' I added for good measure.

*Sometimes when things are embarrassing, the best thing you can do is make a joke. And if you've ever made someone really laugh, you'll know that it's one of the best feelings in the world. After eating gelato, of course.

This made him laugh even harder.

'Here, Enid, you try.' I handed her the ball.

She took it and started bouncing it as though she had been doing it her whole life.

'Nice one! You got it!' said Connor.

'Well, we *do* have a hoop at home, so I've had a little bit of practice,' said Enid.

*What? Enid can already play? I'm the only noob here?*

My heart sank, along with any hope of getting out of this with my dignity and possibly kneecaps intact.

Enid saw my face and said, 'You'll get the hang of it, Melody. Try again!'

This time I bounced it so gently that it just stayed down there on the ground. I felt like joining it. Maybe we could take a nap together. Watch a movie. Anything but this.

'Bit harder. Split the diff!' said Rebecca.

I tried again and this time the ball actually came back up, which took me by surprise, so I wasn't ready to hit it again and had to just watch it go off on its own special journey. Connor grabbed it, though, and bounced it back to me.

'That's it, Melody, you're getting it!' he said encouragingly.

I reached out and bounced it again.

And again!

I managed about three before it got away from me, but the others came in and bounced it back and soon we were all bouncing the ball like it was a real live game of basketball!

We spent the next half-hour like that. Just bouncing the ball around the court and laughing. It was actually heaps of fun! I never knew sport could be fun.

*Colour me surprised!*

Eventually, the groundskeeper came to lock the court, so we packed up our stuff and all walked to the bus stop together.

'Thanks so much for teaching us, you guys,' I said as Connor's bus pulled up. 'That was cool!'

'Hey, you're a natural!' Connor replied, flashing me a smile as he got on the bus. He practically had to duck.

*Surely this tall Year 8 boy couldn't actually like little-old short-stuff nerdo me?*

'Hey, wait for me, silly!' said Rebecca, jumping on the bus with him.

Enid and Rebecca caught the same bus as me, so why was Rebecca getting on Connor's bus?

Then I realised.

*Oh.*

***Oh, I see.***

'See you at home!' called Rebecca to her sister.

As the bus took off, I felt so ridiculous. Of course, Connor and Rebecca were together! Year 8 kids aren't interested in Year 7 kids!

'Connor's so lovely, isn't he?' she said.

'Oh, yeah. He's nice,' I agreed.

*Too nice for the likes of me.*

Then Enid turned to me and said excitedly, 'So, what

do you think? Should we join the basketball club?'

'Maybe. I don't think I'm ready yet.'

'I'll see if Bec and Connor will give us another lesson.'

*Please no.*

'Great,' I said, trying to sound cheerful.

'It was fun, hey?'

'Yeah. Heaps fun.' That much was actually true.

'As fun as musical theatre?' asked Enid, smiling.

'In a different way. It was like I didn't have any thoughts or worries when we were playing. Like my brain switched off.'

'That's what I love about sport,' she said. 'You can just get lost in the moment.'

'I never thought about it like that,' I said.

I sure did get lost in the moment.

*Silly Melody Moss.*

# CHAPTER 7: Chocolate Prawns

Saturday, 3 May
8.40pm

Mum made chocolate prawns tonight. It's a Spanish thing, apparently.

'Here's our Michael Jordan!' said Dad when I sat down.

'Who?' I asked.

'Only the greatest basketball player of all time! Come *on*!' He pretended to shoot a ball into the top of the microwave.

'Thirty years ago,' Mum scoffed at him. Then she turned to me. 'So? How was it?'

'It was actually quite fun. Enid's sister and another Year 8 kid were teaching us. They asked us to join the basketball club.'

'You'll be busy! Basketball *and* musical theatre,' said Dad. 'What a combo!'

'Like prawns and chocolate,' said Ash sarcastically.

Mum inspected her food, worried. 'Is it **weird?** It's weird, isn't it?'

'I like it!' said Dad, tucking in.

'Mum, can Victor and Abby come over tomorrow?' I asked.

Ash groaned.

'For sure!' said Mum.

'Are you and Abby good again now?' asked Dad.

'I guess so. We're all doing musical-theatre club.'

'That's great!' said Mum. 'You guys were always such good friends.'

'Yeah,' I said. 'I mean – we weren't for a while, but she's been nice recently.'

'Maybe she remembered how much fun you guys have together,' said Mum. 'Do Victor and Abby get on?'

'Sort of. Victor is shy and Abby is, you know . . . a lot.'

'You can say that again,' said Ash, rolling her eyes.

'Don't be a grumpy-bum, Ashley,' Dad said with a wink. Ash poked out her tongue at him.

'I'll think of something special for lunch,' said Mum.

*Yikes.*

'Thanks, Mum.'

Ash smirked.

'Anyway, I think it's great, the basketball thing,' said Dad. 'You said you were going to broaden your interests and you're doing it. You have to take a few risks in life, otherwise it would be boring and predictable. Unlike these chocolate prawns.'

9.15pm

I was just watching *High School Musical* – because it has a song about basketball; whoever said musical theatre and sport couldn't go together – when my phone pinged.

A text from Abby:

check your emails

I checked my emails and there was one from Miss Elliot!

*For all those interested in Musical Theatre Club, we will have our first get-together on Tuesday after school in the music room. Look forward to seeing you all then!*

I texted Abby back:

OMG

Exciting

IKR?

See you tomorrow!

XXXXXXXXXX

*Oh, that's right. Abby is invading my afternoon with Victor.*

***Dang it.***

I'm sure it will be fine. It's just three kids hanging out on a Sunday afternoon.

Absolutely no reason to stress about tomorrow.

**Tomorrow should be absolutely fine.**

# CHAPTER 8: Tomorrow

Sunday, 4 May
9.14am

Goals for this afternoon:

- Make Victor join the musical theatre club whether he likes it or not.
- Get Victor to actually talk about 'The Visitors'.
- Keep Abby from annoying the hell out of both of us.

Seems manageable.

## 7.53pm

Luckily, Victor arrived before Abby. I answered the door and pulled him inside.

'We need to talk,' I said, with my Serious Face on.

Once we were safely in my room and out of earshot, I sat him down and gave him **The Look**.

'What?' he asked.

'Are you going to join musical-theatre club or not?'

'Maybe.'

'OMG, Victor, you're killing me! You've gotta save me from Abby!'

'You'll be okay. She *was* your best friend, after all.'

'But *you're* my best friend now, Victor. Besides, we haven't talked about the **other thing**.' I nodded towards the wardrobe.

'Yeah. That was weird.'

'I don't get why you can see them now too.'

'I'm hoping it was a one-off,' he said.

'**Two**-off.'

'Look,' he said, 'I don't have time for imaginary musical-theatre characters at the moment. Piano is getting really intense.'

'I don't think we have much choice, Victor.'

'Why do you think they come?' he asked. 'Maybe if we can work that out, we can find a way to stop them?'

'They usually show up when I have a problem, to give me advice.'

'Maybe it's just a "you" thing. I've only ever seen them here, in your room. Do you see them anywhere else?'

'Well, yes. There was the mermaid who visited me in the girls' toilets last term. That got me in a whole world of trouble, as you know.'

'Do you *want* them to stop?'

I'd never really asked myself this.

'Yes . . . No . . . I don't know. I want to understand why you can see them now.'

'Maybe they're trying to tell me something too,' he said.

'Like what?'

'Like I should stop hanging around *you*, for a start!' He laughed and gave me a playful shove.

'Nah, you love me,' I said, laughing.

I had started to tickle him, which made him squeal and made Toto very barky, when the doorbell rang.

'Buckle up,' I said. 'Here she is.'

Victor took a deep breath, and I ran to answer the door. But I was too late. Ash had got there before me.

***Oops!***

She opened the door to Abby, who was dressed from head to foot in purple. Like an eggplant.

'Hi Ash!' said Abby, beaming.

Ash took one look at her and turned around without saying a word.

## Rude.

But Abby was unbothered and as soon as she saw me she said, 'Melody! Squeeeee!'

Ash put her hands over her ears as she walked up the stairs and back to her Cave of Doom.

'Come to my room,' I said. 'Victor's already here.'

'Amazing! I have jumbo snakes and sour worms,' she said, holding them up like weapons of defence.

When we walked into my room, Victor was sitting on my bed, staring, with the strangest look on his face.

I looked in the direction he was staring and saw her.

*A small child just standing there.*

In my room.

She looked like a kid from the olden days, a bit grubby and a bit naughty. She had a big grin on her face and gave a little wave to me that sent chills up my spine.

***Oh no!***

***Not now!***

***Not in front of Abby!***

'Actually, let's get food!' I said, quickly turning Abby back around towards the door.

'But I have snakes!' she protested.

In the blink of an eye, the little girl had crawled across the floor and was standing in front of the door, blocking our exit and giggling!

'Don't panic!' I shouted at Abby. 'I can explain!'

'Why would I panic?' said Abby, clearly confused.

I looked at her and realised that **she couldn't see the girl**. Victor was still sitting on the bed, his mouth open in horror.

'Stop being weird, Melody. Let's just open the lollies,' said Abby, tearing open the packet.

As soon as she opened it, the little girl stuck her hand in it, grabbed several snakes, then ran over to the wardrobe and climbed on top to devour them.

Abby didn't notice a thing.

*Only Victor and I can see the girl.*

*This is good. This is okay. I can work with this.*

*Maybe if we just ignore her, she'll go away.*

'I'll have a snake,' I said. Abby offered me the packet and I took a couple, but obviously not the orange ones because, even in a crisis, they are still the worst flavour.

'Victor. Have a snake,' I said, making strong eye contact to say, *act normal.*

Victor nodded, his eyes still on the little girl, and took a snake.

'Oh, Victor, of course you like the orange ones!' said Abby, laughing.

The little girl then **threw a snake at Victor**.

***Victor screamed.***

Abby jumped.

Victor was totally freaking out, swiping at himself like it was a real snake.

'What the hell, Victor – are you okay?' said Abby in shock.

'SNAKE!' was all Victor could say.

The little girl laughed and jumped off the cupboard, then started running in circles around the room. Each time she passed Victor, she poked him with her finger and giggled.

It would have been cute if it wasn't

ABSOLUTELY

TERRIFYING.

*Ignore her, Melody! This kid isn't the boss of you!*

'So . . . Abby?' I asked, leaning casually on the desk. 'Do you want to look up what musicals are on at the moment?'

'Sure,' said Abby, sitting on my desk chair.

While she was looking at her phone, Victor was making very serious 'help' faces at me.

The little girl wandered over to Abby and looked curiously at her phone, as though she'd never seen one.

'So . . . there's *Oliver*,' said Abby, scrolling.

'I love *Oliver*. Don't you, Victor?' I asked, trying to seem relaxed, like everything was okay.

Victor was not okay.

'Um . . . yep, it's pretty good, I guess,' he said, with his eyes on the girl.

'And *Annie* is also on,' said Abby, excited. 'That's one of your favourites, isn't it, Melody?'

'Oh yes, I love *Annie*! All those funny little orphan girls.'

The little girl looked at me sharply. It seemed she did *not* like the sound of that. Next thing I knew, she'd snatched the phone out of Abby's hand and thrown it across the room, narrowly missing Victor's head!

'**What the heck**, Melody! What did you *do* that for?' asked Abby, astonished.

'I . . . I didn't . . .' I stammered.

The little girl looked cross and stood there with her arms folded.

'Oh, I suppose the phone just threw itself across the room, did it?' said Abby.

'It's fine. Look, it landed on the bed,' I said, going over to get it.

Then the little girl stuck her foot out and tripped me and I fell on top of Victor, both of us in a screaming heap.

'Whoa! Are you guys okay?' asked Abby, stunned. 'What on earth is going on?'

I scrambled to my feet and grabbed Abby's phone. As I turned to give it to her, I saw that the little girl was *standing on my desk, holding my fishbowl over Abby's head!*

'I'm **STARVING**!' shouted Victor suddenly.

*Victor to the rescue!*

'Oh, me too!' I shouted back. 'Sorry, Abby, I think I'm a bit light-headed. I skipped breakfast. Let's go have some lunch.'

Victor rushed over to open the bedroom door. I pushed Abby towards it, out of harm's way. Then I turned around to grab the fishbowl off the little girl . . .

**. . . but she was gone!**

The bowl was sitting back on my desk, Spike looking as normal as can be expected for a goldfish who spends every day swimming around a tiny, pink, plastic Eiffel Tower.

I followed Abby and Victor out of the room, but as I closed the door behind me, I heard a little mischievous giggle from inside.

'MUM!' I called down the hallway. 'Can we have lunch now?'

Mum appeared at the kitchen doorway looking thrilled.

'I hope you kids are hungry!' she said, beaming.

*One of Mum's fancy cooking experiments has never been more welcome.*

'We're starving!' I replied.

We spent the rest of the afternoon in the living room. I wasn't going to risk returning to my bedroom till Abby was gone. The three of us got very excited by the thought of seeing *Oliver* or *Annie* and sang along to all the songs, which made Mum smile and Ash leave the house.

8.30pm

Back in my bedroom now. Just me, Toto and her farts.

*Keep farting, Toto! We need to smoke them out of here!*

What a day! **Sheesh!**

# CHAPTER 9: Birthday Countdown

Monday, 5 May
5.17am

I just woke up in a **panic**. It's my thirteenth birthday in two weeks and I haven't planned anything!!

What do teenagers do for their birthdays? In primary school, you either invite the whole class to your house, or you go to the zoo or something with one or two besties.

I'm in high school now, I can't go to the flipping zoo!

Okay. I just googled 'thirteen-year-old birthday party ideas'.

- Pool Party: I don't think so. It's the middle of winter and we would all become Instant Human Icicles. Also, we don't have a pool.
- Laser Tag: Running around shooting each other? I think not, Google.
- Escape Room: This is already my life.
- DIY Craft Party: Or 'How to become a Social Outcast again in one short step'.
- Movie Night: Getting warmer, Google, getting warmer . . .
- Karaoke: Bingo! This is the one! All my friends can sing along with me to my favourite musical-theatre songs! Nailed it, Google!

Now I just have to wait several hours till Mum wakes up to ask her!

7.30am

She said yes!

She's going to ask Dad to organise it because he's a musician and can get all the sound equipment. And she's going to make us 'really interesting food'. *gulp*

Now I just have to figure out who to invite.

*Way to turn the morning around, Melody Moss.*

And to top it all off – it's our first meeting of musical-theatre club after school!

**Wheeeeeee!!**

8.10pm

I bumped into Victor walking into school and told him my exciting news.

He didn't seem very excited.

I'd forgotten that even though Victor has an amazing singing voice, he's extremely shy – karaoke would be an actual nightmare for him.

*How can I have a party that my best friend won't enjoy?*

'That's okay,' he said. 'I can just watch everyone else sing. I don't mind.'

'But Victor, the singing is the fun part! I don't even have a good voice like you but I'm going to do it!'

'But Melody, you have one thing I don't have.'

'What's that?'

'Confidence.'

He was right. Victor is super shy. And for no reason, because he's talented and funny and smarter than most people I know.

'Well, maybe you can sing a duet with me? Just one? For my birthday? Pleeeeeease?' I made a pathetic little pleading face.

'I'll think about it,' he said with the smallest glimmer of a smile.

*That's as good as a yes.*

Somehow, I got through Mrs Butcher's Science class about the force of gravity – which was certainly having an effect on my eyelids after waking up so early – and managed to drag myself through to lunchtime.

'So, guys . . .' I said, once everyone was gathered in our spot. 'I have some very exciting news.'

When I had their full attention, I continued. 'It's my birthday in two weeks and I've decided to have a . . .'

*Pause for dramatic effect.*

**'Karaoke party!'**

I may have oversold it, because I really did not get the reaction I'd hoped for.

'Cool,' said Abby.

'Yeah,' said Victor.

Enid and Epiphany didn't say anything.

'Well, you know I'm not much of a singer . . .' said Tyler.

'Guys! The whole point of karaoke is just to have fun! It's actually **more fun** if you're not a good singer. We can all laugh at each other!'

'That doesn't sound very nice,' said Abby, 'laughing at each other.'

*This is not how I imagined it going down.*

'We'll be laughing at **ourselves**, Abby. You know – not taking ourselves too seriously.'

'I take my singing *very* seriously, Melody. I'm actually considering a career as a singer, and I don't really want people laughing at me.'

***OH,***

***FOR***

***CRYING***

***OUT***

***LOUD!***

'What about basketball?' said Enid.

WHAT? NO!

Shut up, Enid!

'You were saying the other day how much fun you had,' she continued. 'You could have a basketball party.'

'That sounds cool!' said Tyler.

'I'd like to learn!' said Epiphany.

'Sure, why not,' said Abby, clearly happy for the change of tack.

I looked at Victor for help.

'Hmm . . . Karaoke or basketball? I couldn't possibly choose,' he said dryly.

*Thanks a lot, Victor.*

So much for turning my morning around.

'Okay, well, thanks for that feedback, *everyone*,' I said. 'I will . . . think about it.'

Then I opened my beetroot hummus and pickled anchovy wrap, which smelled extreme and made a few people frown and look around for the source. It was a perfect ending to a super awkward conversation.

8.24pm

Texts to Victor:

Please tell me you're coming to musical-theatre club tomorrow

I don't know

I've gotta practise piano

Just this once

If it sux, you don't have to come again

🙏🙏🙏🙏🙏

Okay, okay

I'll see you there

Yay

See you tomorrow

🤍🤍🤍🤍🤍

# CHAPTER 10: Musical Theatre Club

Tuesday, 6 May
6.26pm

Once the bell rang after a particularly fascinating two hours of Maths and History – *not* – I ran to the music room.

The music room is like my sanctuary. The cosiest place in the school by far. Miss Elliot was waiting at her desk, and I was the first person there.

'Goodness, did you run here, Melody?' she said, laughing.

Abby arrived next and came to sit beside me. Then Maud, who was in our musical last term as a Very

Serious Pufferfish. Then Zach, who played Daddy Octopus. Then a couple of kids from Year 8, including Rebecca followed by . . . Enid. I thought she wasn't interested in musicals!

*Where's Victor?*

My heart sank.

*He's not going to come.*

Then, just as Miss Elliot was about to start, he finally showed up.

'Don't scare me like that!' I whispered as he sat on the other side of me.

'Sorry! I had to go to the bathroom.'

'Ew, Victor. TMI.'

Miss Elliot got us to sit in a circle on the floor, which made it feel less like school and more like fun.

'Let's go around the circle and introduce ourselves

and share what we like about musical theatre. Who would like to go first?'

I shot my hand up. Miss Elliot smiled and said, 'Of course – Melody.'

'Hi, my name's Melody Moss and I've loved musicals since I was little. One day I hope to be a professional writer or a director.' I might have been gushing.

Abby went next. 'My name's Abby. You may recognise me from last term's musical in which I played the lead. I hope to be a professional performer one day, because musicals are *my life*.'

*Hmm . . . This, from a girl who accused me at the start of the year of talking about musicals too much. Backflip much, Abby?*

Victor and I made eye contact and tried not to smirk.

'Hi, I'm Enid. I don't know much about musicals, but I decided to try something new because I was inspired by my friend Melody, here, who has started playing basketball with me.'

*Oh, great. I mean, that's very nice and everything but now I'll have to join the darn basketball club! This is emotional blackmail!*

'Hi, my name is Victor. I play piano. I like musicals because . . .'

He looked really nervous, and I wanted to help him.

*You got this, Victor.*

'Because . . . I guess I have always felt like an outsider, and musicals make me feel, like, connected. To something. I dunno.'

'That's lovely, Victor,' said Miss Elliot, smiling. 'I think a lot of people feel that way. Theatre does have a way of connecting us all.'

'Hi, I'm Rebecca, Enid's sister. I'm more into sports than plays and stuff, but Enid and I have always done things together, so . . . yeah.'

'Hi, I'm Zach. I was Daddy Octopus in the musical last term. I love singing more than anything, but my mum wants me to be a doctor.'

'Hello, I'm Maud. I'd never been in a play until last term and it was super scary but also exciting and I just really liked coming to rehearsals and being with everyone.'

Then, in the doorway, appeared a very familiar shape. Tall, high backpack, short fringe . . .

Simone, the stage manager from last term's musical!

'Sorry I'm late, Miss E!' she said in her booming voice. 'We had exam prep.'

'That's fine, Simone! We were just introducing ourselves,' Miss Elliot replied.

Simone came and sat in the circle, without taking off her backpack, of course.

*It never comes off.*

'Simone,' she said. 'Year 10, so I may not be able to make every meeting, but yeah. I like the backstage part of theatre. You know, "making it happen". Not really a performer, but good for solving problems. That sort of thing.'

Next, Miss Elliot got us all to talk about our favourite shows. When it was time to finish, I couldn't believe it. It had gone so fast!

'We'll study a different musical each week,' she told us. 'You guys can take turns choosing. Who would like to suggest a show for next week?'

*Be cool, Melody, let someone else have a go.*

'Anyone?' Miss Elliot said, looking right at me.

*My head might explode if someone doesn't say something soon.*

I nudged Victor and glared at him. He looked scared and shook his head slightly.

***Come on, people!***

It was becoming clear that not everyone was as obsessed with musicals as I am. Enid and Rebecca looked stumped. Abby was staring into space; she clearly hadn't been listening.

'Okay, okay!' I blurted out.

'Yes, Melody?' Miss Elliot looked relieved that someone had broken the silence.

I looked at Victor and said, '*West Side Story*'.

'Great suggestion!' she said. 'An absolute masterpiece. Excellent choice, Melody. Now, before we finish, I think we need to come up with a name for this club. Does anyone have any ideas?'

A silence followed, during which:

- Maud's eyes glazed over.
- Victor looked like he was attempting quantum physics.
- Abby bit her lip and looked skyward.
- Zach frowned and drummed his fingers on his shoe.
- My mind whirred at a hundred miles per hour.

*Musicals . . . showtunes . . . Broadway . . . song and dance . . . high school . . . kids . . . babies . . . love . . . appreciation . . . showtime . . . Broadway kids . . . Broadway . . .*

'Broadway Babies!' I shouted, with absolutely no filter whatsoever. Enid jumped and Maud let out a little squeal.

'That's very clever, Melody,' said Miss Elliot, looking impressed. 'From the song "Broadway Baby" by Stephen Sondheim. Does anyone else have a suggestion?'

Nobody did, of course.

Then Miss Elliot played the song 'Broadway Baby'*, which is actually a brilliant song and by the end we were all singing along to it.

*Totes worth a google, especially the Bernadette Peters version. She is an absolute ICON and reminds me a lot of Miss Elliot.

'Okay, then, Broadway Babies,' said Miss Elliot with a massive smile, 'make sure you watch or listen to *West Side Story* before next week. See you then!'

Victor and I walked to the bus stop together, still buzzing from the meeting.

'See, Victor? I told you it would be fun!'

'Thanks for suggesting *West Side Story*,' he said.

'Well, I know it's one of your favourites. But you could have suggested it yourself. Don't let me do all the talking.'

He looked a bit embarrassed. 'I'm sorry. I just get so nervous. I can't help it.'

'Well, maybe this club is exactly what you need, to bring you out of your shell.'

'Maybe.'

Enid and Rebecca joined us at the bus stop.

'Hey guys, did you enjoy it?' I asked them.

'Yeah, it was fun,' said Enid. 'You want to play basketball again on Friday?'

*Absolutely not.*

'Sure!'

'Would you like to play too, Victor?' she asked him.

Victor looked horrified and slightly seasick at the thought.

'Um, no thanks. I've got piano.'

*I don't know what he would do without piano as an excuse for everything LOL.*

'Cool, I'll see if Connor can play too. He's a much better teacher than me,' said Rebecca.

*Oh great – your tall, handsome boyfriend is going to watch me faceplant my way around the court again. Terrific.*

'Yeah, okay, cool,' is what I actually said.

# CHAPTER 11:
# Sporty and Musical

Wednesday, 7 May
5.06am

I woke up very early and **very stressed** because I still haven't figured out my birthday party and it's in **less than two weeks**!

Maybe I can just stay twelve.

Maybe I don't want to be a teenager.

Isn't thirteen meant to be an unlucky number?

I think I'll just skip it.

I can't have a **basketball party**!

## 8.12pm

'I've organised the karaoke machine for your party,' Dad announced over dinner.

*Oh no.*

'Yes, about that,' I said. 'I've been having some second thoughts.'

'Thank the Lord,' muttered Ash.

'What? Why?' asked Mum.

'Because nobody is into it but me. None of my friends. They're not like me, Mum. No-one is. I'm a weirdo.'

'You can say that again,' said Ash.

'Ashley!' scolded Dad.

'Sorry,' she said, clearly not sorry at all.

'Well, what do they all want to do?' asked Mum.

'There seems to be a bit of a push for . . . basketball.'

Ashley nearly choked on her dinner.

'As a party?' Mum was incredulous.

'Yeah. Sounds fun, hey?' I said glumly.

'Well, it's your party, Chicken. You can do whatever you want,' said Dad.

'Maybe you could combine them?' offered Mum.

'Yeah, the world's first karaoke basketball party. You shoot a hoop, then sing a song!' sniggered Ash.

*That's actually not the worst idea I've ever heard.*

'We could put a hoop out the back, set the karaoke machine up outside?' said Dad.

'I can make some Japanese-American fusion food!' Mum added.

'Guys, I wasn't actually serious!' said Ash.

*Actually . . . I love it! It sums up my individual and original personality perfectly!*

'That's it!' I said excitedly. 'Thanks, guys! I'll send out the invites tonight!'

9.16pm

So, I've just finished designing my invite:

Then I addressed it to Victor, Abby, Tyler, Enid (and Rebecca) and Epiphany.

Sent!

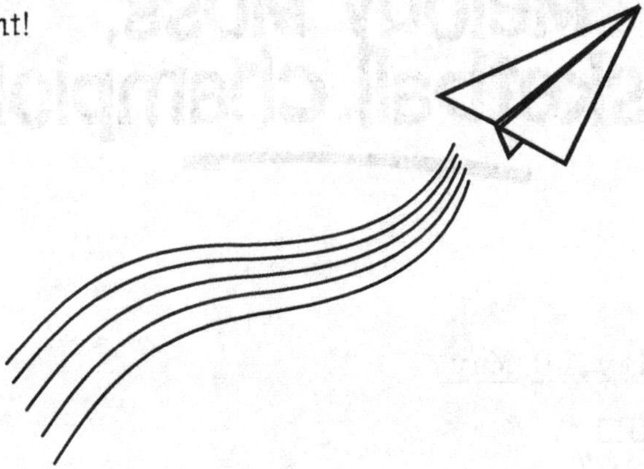

# CHAPTER 12: Melody Moss, Basketball champion

Friday, 9 May
6.12pm

I was a bit pumped walking into school today, having totally nailed my birthday party theme. There's something for everyone! Plus, it's possibly never been done before in the history of birthday parties.

I love being original ☺.

The only thing taking the gloss off was the thought of basketball after school. Even though I'd ended up enjoying myself last week, I still felt self-conscious about my lack of sporting skill, especially in front of Connor. But Enid and Rebecca had showed up to musical-theatre club, so the least I could do was follow through on my promise to explore new things.

In English we're studying genres. I like English, especially when we do creative writing, because creativity is my Weapon of Choice. But it was a very long class with lots of talking from Mrs Bing and it felt like we were all stuck in Historical Fiction with lots of descriptive passages and no action.

**Brriiiinnnnnggg!!!** went the lunch bell. You've never seen a room empty so fast.

Somehow, I got stuck behind the stampede of kids madly escaping the genre lesson. It was like a scene from science fiction.

*See what I did there, Mrs Bing?*

By the time I got to our spot, everyone was already there.

'So, guys,' I said, barely containing my excitement as I opened my blue cheese and cumquat-marmalade sandwich. 'Did everyone get my birthday party invitation last night?'

'Mm-hmm,' said Victor, munching on his sandwich.

'Yep,' said Abby, nodding with her sushi.

Tyler gave a quick thumbs up.

It wasn't complete silence, but it was *not* the response I was expecting.

'Since you guys weren't super keen for karaoke, I thought why not combine karaoke and basketball?! I mean, who's ever done **that?**'

People were actually looking at the grass now.

*What is going on?*

'So, like . . . how will it work?' asked Epiphany.

'Yeah, will it be karaoke for the first half, then basketball?' asked Enid.

'Or, like, both at the same time?' asked Abby, looking confused.

*Oh dear. You really didn't think this through, did you, Melody?*

I looked to Victor for moral support, but he was no help. He knew it was a terrible idea. He just stared at me with raised eyebrows.

*Why didn't I talk to anyone about this before I sent the invitations?*

***It's a completely ridiculous idea!***

## <u>WHAT</u> <u>HAVE</u> <u>I</u> <u>DONE</u>?

So, after that depressing lunch experience, I went through the afternoon very distracted, trying to figure out exactly how my party could work.

Then I realised.

*It can't work!*

*Melody, you fool! Basketball and karaoke are completely different vibes!*

The obvious solution was to do one of them for half the party, then swap.

But that's boring, and Melody Moss is not boring!

Okay. This is a creative challenge! A good theatre director should be able to work out how to make the experience entertaining for all.

Before I knew it, it was bell time, and I had to face the basketball court again. I arrived to find Enid, Rebecca and Connor already there, dribbling.

*Deep breath. It's just a ball, Melody. You can do this.*

'Hi guys!' I said, dumping my bag and walking onto the court.

'Melody!' said Connor. 'Here you go!' And he bounced the ball over to me, which made me panic. I was hoping to ease into the whole thing. I lurched at it, determined, but missed it completely and it bounced away from me, pathetically.

'All good!' he said, retrieving it. 'Maybe we should go into pairs and bounce the ball between us, just to get a feel for it. Melody, do you want to go with me?'

*I mean, obvs.*

It was a confusing combination of emotions: desperately wanting to bounce this ball with this handsome giant of a boy, but also totes nervous about not being able to.

'Um, sure,' I said.

'Cool.' He smiled. Connor had a way about him that was just totally confident and relaxed. I couldn't imagine him being nervous about anything.

Enid and Rebecca went to the other side of the court, while Connor and I stood opposite each other.

'Thanks so much for teaching me how to play,' I said. 'I'm sure there's loads of other things you could be doing on a Friday afternoon.'

'I love it,' he said. 'I'd rather be playing basketball than most things. I'm not great at a lot of stuff other than sport. It's kinda my thing.'

He held the ball up, ready to bounce it towards me.

'Now, are you ready?'

'Um, I think so,' I said.

*I will probably never be ready to have a ball bounced at me.*

'Okay, here we go,' he said and bounced the ball in a completely reasonable way towards me, but it may as well have been a live grenade because for some reason balls coming towards me are terrifying, so I kind of panicked and shielded my face from any potential impact.

*Melody, you absolute derp!*

But Connor didn't laugh, or scoff or anything. He just said, 'That's okay,' and retrieved the ball.

'Why don't you go first?' he said. 'Just aim for the middle between us there, and I'll catch it.'

'I'm so sorry! I've never really played any sports. I'm hopeless!'

'All good! I think it's great you're trying something new. I don't know if I could.'

He passed me the ball and I became aware of how very, very, very tall he was when he was standing only a basketball's distance away from me. It was kind of thrilling.

*Stop it, Melody! This boy is not for you! He's in Year 8! He has a girlfriend!*

***You are not allowed to get a crush on him!***

'Okay, go!' he said. I took a deep breath, looked at him and bounced the ball perfectly, which he caught.

'See? You've got this! You just need to build your confidence. Again.'

We did this a few more times, then, without me noticing, instead of catching the ball, he bounced it back, then I bounced it back and soon we had a whole thing going with the ball bouncing between us like beautiful music.

Enid and Rebecca came over and joined us, and soon we were all drooling together. Sorry – dribbling! We were **dribbling** together LOL.

*Maybe I* **can** *be good at sport! Maybe I have untapped sporting talent just waiting to be discovered!*

***Melody Moss, Basketball Champion!***

Just as I was in the flush of excitement and carefree as a bird, I may have got a little overenthusiastic and one of my feet got stuck behind the other one and next thing I know, my face was **in Connor's chest**!

He made a kind of 'oof' sound.

So many thoughts and emotions went through me in that one split second:

- My face is in his chest.
- His chest is really hard – ow!
- I hope I haven't injured him.
- He smells like laundry powder and apples.
- My nose hurts.
- I must look utterly ridiculous right now.
- I think I'm falling.
- Yep, I'm falling.
- My nose *really* hurts.

Then I slid to the ground.

I sat there, momentarily dazed. My face felt warm and . . . wet? Yes, wet. I put my hand up to my face and when I looked at it I saw red.

*Oh no. A blood nose. This is very bad.*

'Melody!' said Enid. 'Your nose!'

'Hang on, I've got some tissues!' said Rebecca, dashing towards her bag.

'Are you okay?' asked Connor, looking down at me.

'I'm so sorry!' I said to him. 'I hope I didn't hurt you!'

'Not at all,' he replied. 'But you're bleeding . . . quite a lot.'

'Here!' said Rebecca, handing me some tissues.

I pressed them up against my nose.

*What must I look like right now?!*

'Should you call someone to pick you up?' asked Enid.

'Um . . . no. I'm okay. It doesn't really hurt,' I said, even though it totally did.

I cleaned myself up as well as I could. I had blood on my shirt and in my hair, but I was determined to save face.

'I'm fine to catch the bus.'

'Okay, we'll come with,' said Enid.

So, we all stood at the bus stop.

Me, with my head tilted back and still holding a wad of tissues over my nose.

Rebecca suddenly said, 'Oh, hey, thanks for your birthday party invitation! Sounds fun! Basketball *and* karaoke!'

And I suddenly realised something.

*Connor is the only person here I didn't invite!*

## #awks

***What do I do?***

I don't really know him but he's Rebecca's boyfriend and he loves basketball but also I think I've got a crush on him and that's completely ridiculous but I want him to come to my party!

'Oh, you should come too, Connor!' I said, muffled by a mound of bloody tissues.

'Sure, cool. Thanks, Melody. At least I'm good at one of those things!' he said with a laugh.

'Great!' I said, but it came out more like, 'Frake.'

*Great. Real basketball players at my basketball party, which I can't even play without being seriously and humiliatingly injured.*

***What are you thinking, Melody Moss?***

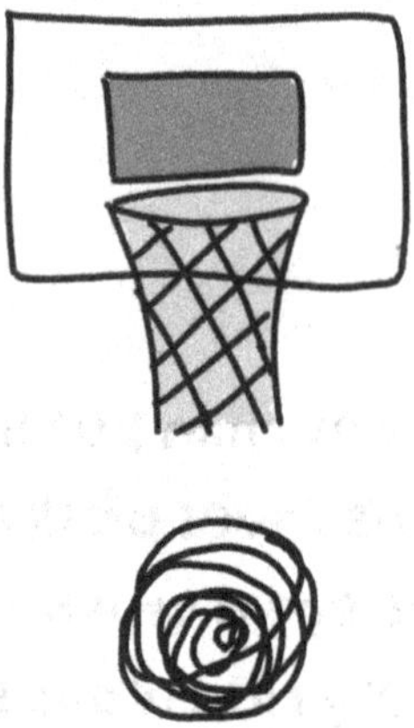

# CHAPTER 13: Denial

Sunday, 11 May
6.12pm

I'd like to say that I've spent the weekend solving the issue of my **Bizarre Birthday Party**, but the truth is, I kind of went into denial and ate a lot of peanut butter on toast.

Did it help?

Yes, it did, and I would do it all over again.

It definitely helped me get over the fact that I arrived home on Friday literally **covered in blood** and feeling like an absolute doofus.

Year 7 is brutal.

And I don't want to alarm anyone, but my birthday party is in *exactly* –

# CHAPTER 14:
# Chill. Relaxed. Unbothered.

Monday, 12 May
6.45am

I have decided that denial is working for me, so I'm just going to be chill about it. I mean, who cares if –

- Nobody comes because it's the stupidest idea ever.
- I make a total fool of myself in front of tall, handsome Connor.
- Everyone is horrifically injured in some kind of basketball incident.
- The party is unbelievably cringe and people hate me forever.

Not me. I don't care at all.

I'm Melody Moss.

Chill. Relaxed. Cool as a cucumber.

Couldn't. Care. Less.

Off to school now. Unbothered.

6.45pm

So, I strutted into school, feeling good about my decision to not let anything bother me.

Morning went well.

Surprise Geography test with Mr Splitz. Well, it was a surprise to *me*. We were apparently told about it on Friday, but I had totally forgotten. So, maybe I didn't remember *all* the answers, having revised nothing but peanut butter toast all weekend, but I think I improvised well.

1) Which Egyptian River is the longest in the world?

- Denial.

2) Name the five oceans.

- Julian, Dick, Anne, George and Timmy.

3) Longest mountain range in the world?

- The Geography Test Mountains.

4) Smallest country by population?

- Ittybittybabyland.

5) Where is the Eiffel Tower located?

- My fishbowl.

6) Does America have crocodiles or alligators?

- No crocs, they all wear sandals.

7) Which Pole is colder – North or South?

- The Icy (Pole).

Nailed it.

Waltz into lunchtime, like, totally chill.

*Wait a minute.*

***Abby and Tyler are in our spot . . .***

***. . . arguing?***

I was at an awkward distance from them, too close to turn around but just close enough to hear what they were saying. So, I got really involved in a loose thread on my school shirt. I was pretending to try to pull it off.

'But you **never** want to do anything I want to do, Tyler!' said Abby. 'What's the point of going out together if we never actually see each other except at school? You won't even do musical-theatre club!'

I stole a glimpse and could see that Tyler was looking at his hands, not saying anything. I felt kind of sorry for him. Abby is a lot.

'Do you even **want** to be my boyfriend anymore?' she asked.

More silence.

*Come on, Tyler, you have to say something!*

At that moment, Abby looked up and saw me. I pretended I'd just arrived.

*Chill. Relaxed. Unbothered.*

'Hi guys, how's it going?' I said with a casual, confident air.

Neither of them said anything.

*This is going to be hard work.*

'So . . .' I said, sitting down. 'You both good for my party on Sunday?'

'I don't know, are we, Tyler?' Abby asked him pointedly.

Tyler looked super uncomfortable.

'Um . . . yeah, totally. I was just saying that I might not do the karaoke part.'

'And I was telling Tyler that he *has* to do the karaoke part because it's a karaoke basketball party and everybody *has* to do both things! Right, Melody?'

*Chill. Relaxed.*

'Well . . . I mean, it will be more fun that way, but if you really don't want to, that's fine too.'

'Well, in that case, I don't want to do the basketball!' said Abby, folding her arms crossly.

*Unbothered.*

'Okay.' I smiled calmly. 'No problem. It's a party, it's meant to be fun. You guys do whatever, I don't mind.'

'Fine,' said Abby, angrily opening her lunch.

'Cool,' said Tyler, clearly relieved the conversation was over.

'Great,' I said, as though my birthday party wasn't turning into a **steaming pile of poo**.

The smoked eggplant and fennel salad Mum had packed me was no help.

When I got home, I cheered myself up by listening to *West Side Story** to prepare for musical-theatre club tomorrow. I suggested the show because it's one of Victor's favourites, so I'm hoping that means he'll actually turn up, even though he said he doesn't want to.

*FYI *West Side Story* is based on *Romeo and Juliet*, but set in New York in the 1950s. The songs are crazy good and it's super sad and I've had a Very Big Cry thinking about star-crossed love**.

**star-crossed love is when people shouldn't be in love with each other for all sorts of reasons (like one of them is in Year 8 and has a girlfriend) but they can't help it.

# CHAPTER 15:
# Peak Victor

Tuesday, 13 May
6.30am

until my party.

Five days to figure out how to combine basketball with karaoke.

At least I have musical-theatre club to look forward to after school. I have decided I should invite everyone from the club to my party.

## 6.47pm

It was a particularly long and boring day of school in which I learned these fascinating and useful things:

- Mrs Butcher has one significantly larger foot. (Does she have to buy two pairs of shoes? What does she do with the leftover ones?)
- If I squeeze my eyes shut really hard, I see stars ***try it*** with the added benefit of staying awake.
- My bag is a Pen-Breaking-Vortex. The minute a pen goes in there it is rendered useless. I have nine non-working pens.
- It's exactly 436 steps from the Science Building to my History class, but 526 steps back again, going *exactly the same route.*

That is how long and boring it was.

I was relieved once the final bell rang so I could get to the music room for the second meeting of Broadway Babies.

Miss Elliot was wearing an especially pretty floral dress. I'm not sure why the music room doesn't smell like all the other rooms in the school, which are all extremely whiffy, but I'm pretty sure it's because of her.

As everyone trickled in, we all sat on the floor like last week. Once everyone was there, I decided to make my announcement.

'Um, guys, before we start, I just wanted to tell you about my birthday party this Sunday. It's a basketball/karaoke theme. You know – sporty *and* musical.'

People looked a bit confused by that but were generally happy to be invited to a party, I think.

Then Miss Elliot got us to go around the circle and name our favourite song from *West Side Story*. A few people hadn't listened to it and weren't prepared, but seeing as it's a club and not actual school, Miss Elliot didn't mind.

- Simone the Stage Manager chose 'Gee, Officer Krupke' because it's really funny. I didn't realise she had such a sense of humour. She is a constant surprise.
- Abby chose 'Somewhere' and had actually learned the song to sing for us. Miss Elliot accompanied her on the piano and even though Abby is a total show-off, I had to admit that it was really good.
- I chose 'Jet Song'* as my favourite, because I love the dancing in the movie. When Miss Elliot played it for us, we couldn't help but get up and dance, and by the end, everybody was dancing all over the room and singing along. It was the actual best.

When it was Victor's turn to choose, he kind of froze.

*Google 'Jet Song' and try to remain completely still – I dare you.

***Come on, Victor!***

Even when it's something he knows so much about, he still hasn't got the confidence to speak up. I was just about to suggest a song for him, when I saw something out of the corner of my eye.

***Oh no.***

***Not here.***

The little girl who visited us the other day in my bedroom.

In the music room!

She was hiding behind the piano. Then I saw her reach a little arm out and hit a couple of keys. Tinkle, tinkle. Like she was playing a game with us.

I looked nervously at Miss Elliot, but she didn't seem to have heard anything. Nobody did, except Victor, who had turned as white as a sheet.

'Victor?' asked Miss Elliot again. 'Do you have a favourite song?'

Victor was frozen in time and space. Possibly transported to another dimension, from the look on his face.

'Victor!' I said through clenched teeth.

It was getting really awkward. Everyone was waiting for him to say something.

I followed his gaze and saw that the little girl had now brazenly walked out from behind the piano, had sat on the piano stool and raised both of her hands high in the air, about to crash them down on the keys!

***Is nobody else seeing this?***

'AMERICA!' Victor suddenly shouted, startling everyone. Maud let out a little yelp of shock. And then, almost in slow motion, I watched as he ran over towards the piano as the girl's hands were about to hit the keys and he bumped her off the stool and started playing 'America' from *West Side Story*.

Not only did he play it, **he sang it as well!**

This was the least Victor-y thing I've ever seen Victor do. He was like a boy possessed! Like he was playing for his life! The little girl was absolutely delighted and started dancing in front of him with all the choreography from the movie.

If I hadn't seen it with my own eyes, I would never have believed it.

By the time he was finished, the little girl had run off and everyone in the room was **absolutely floored**.

'That was . . . **amazing**, Victor,' said Miss Elliot. 'How special to have you perform that for us. You must've worked very hard on it.'

Victor was flushed and looked kind of unhinged. His hair was all messed up and he had worked up a sweat.

'Actually, I've been playing that one since I was five,' he said shyly.

*Peak Victor.*

When club was over, Victor and I walked to the bus stop together, talking in hushed tones. He seemed really shaken.

'What the hell, Melody? What was that kid doing there? I thought this stuff only happened in your room!'

'No, I said it had happened here at school before. A mermaid jumped out of the toilet, remember?'

'Okay, gross. But look . . . I don't think I can do this anymore, Melody. It's too much.'

***Uh-oh, this isn't good.***

'What do you mean?' I asked.

'This stuff only happens when I'm around you. And it freaks me out.' He looked really upset. 'I think I need to stay away from you for a while.'

*No, not again.*

*Not Victor.*

'But Victor, look what happened. You were amazing in there, playing and singing. It was like a totally different Victor! Old Victor would never have done something like that!'

He wheeled around on me, not even bothering to be quiet anymore.

'There *is* no Old Victor! It's just me! Normal Victor! I don't want to be different! I like my quiet life. I don't want to be a performer, or hang with lots of musical-theatre people, or be haunted by made-up characters that have come to life. I just want to be alone and play piano.'

***I can't believe this is happening.***

'But Victor, you're my best friend.'

He looked really sad, but clearly he had made up his mind.

'I'm sorry, Melody. I just need a break.'

He turned and walked towards the bus stop, which was awkward because I was going there too. So, I just stood there for a bit, feeling lost and confused, not knowing what to do.

Just at that moment, Enid and Rebecca walked up.

'Hey Melody,' said Enid. 'That was totally awesome! We're loving Broadway Babies. I didn't know everyone was so talented. What about Victor?!'

'Yeah,' I said, trying to force a smile. 'He's awesome.'

'Are you up for some basketball again on Friday?' asked Rebecca. 'You gotta get some practice in before your party on Sunday. How's that going to work, by the way?'

## ***PLEASE JUST SHUT UP!***

'I, ah . . . it's a surprise!' I said. This is a technique I learned from my mum. If you don't know the answer to something, just say it's a surprise.*

*It obviously doesn't work for every question, like 'Where did you put my keys?' or 'Is Fluffy going to pull through?'

'Okay, cool,' said Rebecca. 'Well, see you on Friday? Might be time to shoot some actual hoops, hey?'

*Oh God. That's right. You have to get the ball in the really high baskety thing.*

'Yes!' I said, trying to look sporty. 'Can't wait to do **that**!'

Then we all arrived at the bus stop where Victor was waiting, and it was totes awks.

I am now at home under my *Annie* doona cover, with Toto.

This is the second time a best friend has dumped me this year.

And my birthday is in **five days**.

# CHAPTER 16: Down the S Bend

Wednesday, 14 May
7.30pm

I really didn't want to go to school today, but I was kind of hoping that Victor would –

- have changed his mind about not being friends anymore,
- say he didn't mean any of it,
- beg me to accept his apology, which I would graciously do.

None of that happened.

In fact, Victor didn't come to school today. He must be really upset.

I dragged my sad little self into English. Mrs Bing had us write haikus.*

This was mine:

Birthday party's soon
and yet I feel despondent.
Wish I could just Not.

Luckily, she didn't get me to read it out in class like Stella. Hers was even more depressing:

I am but a sheet
Of toilet paper floating
Right down the S bend.

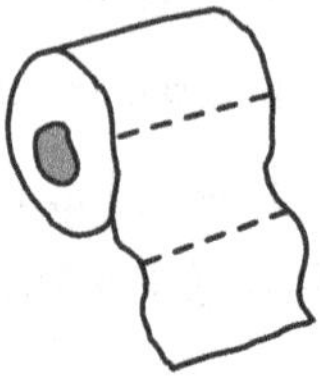

Year 7 is definitely starting to take its toll.

*A haiku is a Japanese poem with five syllables, seven syllables, then five syllables. They can be useful if you need to express yourself but you're short on time.

I made my way, sadly, to our spot for lunch, where I knew there would be no Victor because his classmate, Harry, had already told me he was sick.

I joined Enid and Epiphany to have my lunch. It was unusually quiet.

'Where are Abby and Tyler?' I asked.

Enid and Epiphany gave each other a weird look.

'What?' I asked.

'Should we tell her?' Enid asked Epiphany.

'She's going to find out anyway,' said Epiphany.

'Find out **what?**' I asked.

*I really don't need any more bad news today.*

Enid looked at me for a second, then checked to see if anyone was nearby, before saying dramatically, 'Abby and Tyler have broken up.'

## *ABBY AND TYLER HAVE BROKEN UP.*

If I had heard those words last term, I would have been over the moon. But now, all I could think was:

***My birthday party is in four days' time!***

'What? When?' I asked.

Epiphany, looking slightly pleased, decided this was her moment to shine.

'Well . . .' she said, 'apparently after Broadway Babies last night, Abby rang Tyler to tell him how she sang really well, and he should have been there to support her, and he said that he didn't really want all the pressure of having a girlfriend right now and so they broke up.'

Then Enid took over. 'Abby is totally devo, so she stayed home from school.'

'What about Tyler?' I asked.

'I think he's over there playing football,' said Enid.

I looked towards the oval and recognised the familiar figure of Tyler playing football with some other boys. He looked happier than I've ever seen him.

*Good for you, Tyler.*

8.18pm

Texts to Abby:

Sorry about you and Tyler

Hope you're ok

♡♡♡

THNX

ILL BE OK

CU TOMORROW

💔

Texts to Victor:

Missed you at school today

Hope you're ok

Can we talk?

No response.

☹

# CHAPTER 17: Pity Party

Thursday, 15 May
5.13pm

Victor was at school today, but he was nowhere to be seen at lunch.

Same with Tyler.

Abby was there, though. It was one big **Pity Party** in our spot.

'I just think I deserve better, you know?' she said, sniffling.

'Oh, **totally**,' said Epiphany.

'Like, performing is my **thing**. We got together doing a show but now he doesn't even want to hear me sing, or anything. It was like false pretences, you know? Like he tricked me into believing he was something he's not.'

'Maybe you're just really different people,' I offered.

Abby looked at me for a moment, then burst into tears.

'We **are**!' she wailed. 'It's so tragic, because we were, like, drawn to each other, but we just have such different interests.'

'You're exactly like Maria and Tony from *West Side Story*!' said Enid, thrilled with herself.

'OMG, we *are*!' cried Abby.

***This.***

***Is.***

***Torture.***

*I wish Victor was here.*

*And what the heck is in my sandwich?*

I never figured it out. By the end of lunch, I was very happy to get back to class.

# CHAPTER 18: chaos

Friday, 16 May
5.23am

Woke up in **HYSTERICS** because my birthday party is in –

And:

- My best friend isn't talking to me.
- My former best friend and my former crush aren't talking to each other.
- I have a *totally random* party theme involving basketball.
- I cannot play basketball.

Total and utter disaster.

I need help.

I need a lifeline.

I need someone who is good in a crisis.

*Who do I know who is good in a crisis?*

I know . . .

<u>SIMONE</u> <u>THE</u> <u>STAGE</u> <u>MANAGER</u>.

I am going to find her today and tell her everything. Maybe, she will be able to save me.

Oh, and I have basketball this afternoon.

**Aaaaggghhhhh!!!!**

8.30pm

I saw Victor in the hallway between classes this morning.

'Hi!' I said, smiling.

'Hi,' he said, not.

'Are you still coming to my party?' I asked anxiously.

'I'm not sure, Melody.' He looked really sad. 'I'm nervous to be around you. You seem to attract chaos.'

I mean, he wasn't wrong.

'Please come, Victor. It won't be the same without you! Everything's turned to poo. Abby and Tyler have broken up, so I don't even know if they're coming.'

'See?' he said, shrugging. 'Chaos.'

'It's not *my* fault they broke up,' I said indignantly.

'Maybe not, but somehow this stuff seems to happen around you.'

He turned to go.

'That's not very fair, Victor.'

He couldn't even look at me.

'Sorry. That's just how I feel. I've gotta get to class.'

And off he went.

*So, that happened.*

At lunchtime I went on a mission to find Simone the Stage Manager.

I tentatively crept into the Year 10 area.

*Yikes, these kids are big!*

They were all studying and looking very important and distracted.

'Um, hi, have you guys seen Simone?' I asked nervously.

'Ah, yeah, she's usually in the hall on Fridays,' said one boy who looked old enough to fly a 747.

I went to the hall and found Simone there, setting up a microphone and speakers, wearing her trademark High Backpack.

'Simone. I need your help,' I said pathetically.

She looked at me, then put down the cable she was winding around her arm and sat on the edge of the stage.

'What's up, Melody Moss? You look too stressed for Year 7. Musical-theatre crisis?'

Something in the kind way she looked at me made all the emotions well up inside me and before I knew it, tears were streaming down my face as I told her the whole sorry story – apart from the small child dancing around the music room, of course.

'Okay,' she said. 'First things first. You can't control what other people do. If Victor and Abby and Tyler all have their own dramas and don't come to your party, that's their problem. What you **can** control is how awesome your party is going to be. And **that** I can help you with.'

'You can?' I said, sniffling.

She got straight down to business. 'Here's what I'll do. I'm going to come to your house on Sunday morning and we'll set everything up and make a plan. Don't you worry, Melody Moss.'

I felt a huge wave of relief wash over me.

'Thank you, Simone!'

'No worries. Now get outta here. I've got cables to organise.'

Then I walked to our lunch spot to find Abby, Enid and Epiphany sitting around, looking Generally Emotional.

'Hey Melody,' sighed Abby.

'How are you feeling?' I asked her, not really wanting to know.

'Oh, you know. Heartbroken. Can you believe he hasn't even called me?'

'But you guys broke up . . .' I said, like a fool.

'Yes, but I'm not **DEAD**. I still have **FEELINGS**. After all we've been through together, he doesn't even bother to ask how I am.'

'Do you know if he's coming to my party on Sunday?' I said, like an even bigger fool.

'He'd better not be, or **I'm not coming**!' she wailed.

Enid and Epiphany both put an arm around her sympathetically.

'Right, well, I'm sure he's not. I'll check,' I said.

*Got to find Tyler.*

He was playing football on the oval with some other boys again.

At the start of the year, I thought all boys were Smelly, Dumb, Gross and Of No Useful Purpose. Then I met Victor and Tyler and realised that boys are actually human beings, just like girls.

***Who knew?***

A lot of them don't smell and some of them are quite useful. And very occasionally, one of them can be drop-dead unbelievably gorgeous, like Tyler.

I watched for a few minutes as he kicked the ball around. It always seemed to me like such a pointless thing to do. But since I've been playing basketball, I have started to see that sport can actually be fun.

Once he saw me, he came over.

'Hey,' he said, smiling.

'Hey. Sorry to interrupt.'

'S'cool. We were just mucking about.'

'Avoiding Abby?' I asked.

He winced. 'Um, yeah. Kinda. I think she's mad at me.'

'I think she's upset.'

'Yeah.'

'Yeah. Um . . . *on* that. I was just wondering if you were still coming to my party on Sunday. I get it if it's too awkward now you and Abby have broken up . . .'

'Well . . . I'd really like to come, but I don't want to upset anyone.'

He was so reasonable, so mature, so kind, that something in me sort of snapped.

*Abby doesn't get to tell me who can come to my own birthday party!*

'Actually, Tyler, I came to tell you that I'd still really like you to come. Don't worry about Abby. She'll be fine.'

Relief and excitement spread over his handsome face.

'Seriously? Okay, cool. I love basketball. Not so sure about karaoke, but it could be funny, hey?'

Tyler singing is **always** funny.

'Definitely,' I replied. 'See you on Sunday, then.'

'See ya, Melody.' And he flashed me one of those killer Tyler smiles that made my heart, and possibly my face, completely melt.

Mrs Butcher's class on climate change only added to my anxiety. As if I wasn't feeling doomed enough, we are apparently several degrees away from incineration. Thanks a lot!

After school I made my way to the basketball courts, because apparently this is what I do on Fridays now, like some sort of Sportswoman.

Rebecca and Connor were there already, 'shooting hoops'. They're both pretty good at getting the ball in the high baskety thing, but they are also both **tall**.

The only way I'm getting the ball in there is if one or more of the followings things happen –

- A conveniently timed gust of wind shoots it up out of my hands.
- A large, helpful bird grabs it and drops it in.
- I do some elaborate ladder work faster than the naked eye can see.
- A huge and explosive fart propels me up there.

'Are you ready to play some basketball?' asked Enid, walking up.

'I guess. It's very high, isn't it?' I said, worried.

'It's all about angles,' Enid replied. 'I'm not very good at it yet either. It's really fun when you get it in, though,' she added with a grin.

Connor and Rebecca were super patient with me as I tried and tried to get the ball in the really high baskety thing. But it was no use. I couldn't even get the ball *near* it! Enid got it in a couple of times, and I could see how happy that made her.

Then Connor said, 'Try this,' and he held his arms out in front of him in a circle like a hoop. 'See if you can just get it in there.'

'But what if it hits you in the face?' I said, horrified.

'Don't worry about my face.'

*He clearly has not seen his face.*

So, I stood a few metres away and held the ball in my hands. I looked at the circle he made with his arms, then up to his face, which was so pleasingly un-smashed-in right now.

'You can do it,' he said, making impossibly intense eye contact with me.

I looked at his arms.

I looked at his face.

I held up the ball.

I gently tossed the ball.

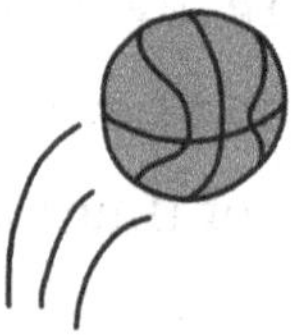

***It went right in!***

Yes, he may have moved slightly to help. But still – I'll take that as a win!

'Okay! Bit further back!' he said, moving a few paces away from me.

I got it in again! And this time he didn't even have to help me!

Enid and Rebecca cheered. It was *so* satisfying.

We did that a few more times until I got confident with it.

'Okay, let's try the hoop again,' he said. 'Watch what I do.'

He held the ball, looking at the hoop, then effortlessly tossed it through. Then he passed it to me.

'Look at the hoop, not the ball,' he said.

'Imagine it going in. It's all about confidence,' said Rebecca.

'You got this, Melody!' said Enid.

I looked at the hoop.

I imagined the ball going into it.

I tossed the ball effortlessly . . .

. . . over the fence and into the bushes, where we had to spend five minutes looking for it.

I didn't actually manage to get the ball into the high baskety thing. But I did have fun trying.

'I think you guys are ready to join our basketball club. What do you say?' asked Connor.

'But I can't even get the ball in yet,' I said, embarrassed.

'That's okay,' said Rebecca. 'It's just for fun. We only play among ourselves.'

'Let's do it, Melody. Life can't be all musical theatre!' said Enid.

I had to admit, this was probably the most relaxed hour I'd spent all week. I hadn't even thought about my party. There was no drama. No angst.

The sun was getting low in the sky, and it lit up Connor's sandy hair as he leaned over to pick up his bag. He looked up at me and smiled.

*How many cute-boy smiles can I take in one day?*

'C'mon, you know you want to,' he said with a wink.

***Oh My Actual God I am helplessly in his spell.***

'Okay, okay! I'll do it!' I said, laughing.

'Yay! We play on Thursdays after school,' said Rebecca.

We started walking towards the gate, when Rebecca and Connor peeled away.

'See you guys! We're going to a movie,' said Rebecca.

*Of course they are. That's what Year 8 couples do. Sigh.*

After they left, Enid and I stood at the bus stop in the twilight.

'Rebecca is so nice,' I said. 'I wish my sister was like yours.'

'Isn't your sister nice?' asked Enid.

'She's like a cat. She doesn't have time for mere mortals like me.'

'Well, you can hang with us whenever you like!' said Enid.

'Thanks, Enid. Connor is super nice too. How long have they been going out together?'

'Oh, Connor's not her boyfriend!' laughed Enid.

WAIT.

***WHAT?***

'He's not? But they seem . . .' I couldn't even finish, I was dumbstruck.

'I know. They've been best friends since primary school. Connor lives next door to us, and they were actually born on the same day, can you believe it?'

*No, Enid, I cannot believe it.*

'So, they're just friends?' I asked, incredulous.

'Yeah, they're besties. Like you and Victor,' said Enid.

The mention of Victor was like a record player being scratched by a needle, interrupting my excited thoughts of Connor not having a girlfriend.

*Oh Victor! Don't remind me!*

# CHAPTER 19: Last Day of Being Twelve

Saturday, 17 May

5.06am

How is a girl supposed to sleep when –

- Her thirteenth birthday party is TOMORROW?
- Her best friend might not even be coming?
- She invited her ex-best friend's ex-boyfriend despite being under strict instructions not to?
- She now has TWO cute single boys coming to her party?
- She still hasn't figured out how the party is going to work because it's the stupidest theme ever??

9.13am

I just went into the kitchen to eat my way through a box of Crunchy Nut Corn Flakes, and Ash was in there, drinking an espresso*.

*FYI an espresso is a coffee that is very small and very black, like Ash's heart.

'Are you going to be around for my party tomorrow?' I asked her.

She looked at me for a second, with a slight smirk, then said, 'Your basketball slash karaoke party?'

I immediately regretted having brought it up. 'Yeah. It's going to be **different**, that's for sure!' I tried to laugh it off.

'I'm going to Hannah's for the weekend. I'm also locking my bedroom door. Good luck.'

Sometimes when people say 'good luck' it sounds like they mean exactly the opposite.

What I heard was:

**Your party is doomed to fail, and you only have yourself to blame!**

Which is kind of how I feel, tbh.

Texts with Victor:

please say youre coming to my party

I DONT KNOW MELODY

but youre my bestie

I need you

CAN YOU PROMISE NO 'VISITORS'?

yes

I promise

OK MAYBE

yay

thank you

Oops.

I shouldn't have promised that.

I have no control over **Them**.

**What have I done?**

11.16am

I just came into my bedroom to talk to **Them**.

I stood in the middle of my room and closed my eyes.

'Um . . . guys? I just want to say that even though I'm very grateful for your visits, which are sometimes really helpful and sometimes . . . not, can I please ask that, just for tomorrow, you stay away? Just for one day? Please?'

Nothing. Silence. Just Toto, me and Spike swimming around in circles in his bowl.

I hope **They** heard me.

8.30pm

I just had my last dinner as a twelve-year-old human on this earth.

We had spaghetti bolognese because it's always been my favourite, and I think Mum was feeling emotional about my childhood being over. Also, she was very busy in the kitchen with cooking for tomorrow and she had it in the freezer.

Ash is at her friend's house, so it was just Mum and me, which was kind of nice.

'Are you excited for tomorrow?' she asked over dinner.

***I'M BESIDE MYSELF.***

'Yep.'

'How many are coming?'

'I think around fifteen. All my friends from Broadway Babies, basketball and my usual group of friends.'

'And boys,' she said with a wink.

*Don't remind me. I can't even.*

'Any boys you like?' she asked, pretending way too hard to sound casual.

*Only two of the best-looking boys you've ever seen.*

'Nah, just friends,' I said, not making eye contact.

Thankfully she didn't continue this Beyond Awkward line of questioning.

'Well, your dad will be here in the morning to help set up. It's going to be fun!'

'Oh, and my stage manager friend Simone is coming to help as well.'

'Great!' she said, clearing the bowls away.

I think she could tell I was freaking out a bit. 'You want to help me crumb the chicken katsu?'

So, Mum and I spent the last night of me being twelve crumbing chicken and listening to old songs that she likes from the 80s. I didn't dare play any musical-theatre songs because I didn't want to summon any unwanted visitors.

10.03pm

Turning out my light now.

*Stay away, visitors!*

When I wake up, I will be thirteen.

***Good luck, Teenage Melody Moss!***

(And I mean that sincerely.)

# CHAPTER 20: Thirteen

Sunday, 18 May
9.30pm

**What A Day.**

This is how it started.

I was having the most intense dream . . .

Everyone had come to my party dressed as a different animal. I was trying to explain to Snake Abby that it wasn't an animal theme, while Rabbit Tyler was laughing at me and Moose Victor was running around in circles screaming. Then Emu

Mum started hassling me, saying, 'Darling? It's time to get up. You've slept in. Simone is here.'

Then she shook me gently and, in that moment, I realised that Mum was saying that in real life, and I was still in my bed asleep. I opened my eyes and looked at the clock, which said –

**10.30am!!!!**

***Wait, what, who, where, why?***

My party is in 90 minutes!!!

Simone was standing in my doorway, backpack on, Prepared for Action.

'Mum! Why didn't you wake me earlier? I've never slept this long in my life!' I shrieked, leaping out of bed.

'I guess you needed it. Welcome to being a teenager, sweetheart. Happy Birthday!' said Mum, trying to give me a hug. But I had **no time** for that sort of frivolity.

'**OH MY GOD I'M SO LATE!** I'm sorry, Simone!' I yelled, running around like a wind-up bath toy.

'All good. Get dressed and I'll meet you outside in five,' she said calmly.

'Would you like a coffee, Simone?' I heard Mum ask her as they walked down the hall.

'That'd be awesome, Mrs M, cheers,' Simone replied.

I took a deep breath, then quickly put on the cute blue-and-white netball dress (apparently there's no such thing as a basketball dress, and shorts are not party wear, thank you very much) and new white sneakers I'd bought last weekend, then looked in the mirror.

**Fit Check: tick.** ☑

I went out the back to find Dad setting up the basketball hoop.

'Where do you want to do the karaoke, Peanut?' he asked.

'I don't *know*!' I said, suddenly panicked. I had absolutely zero chill. 'I don't know what I was *thinking*!'

### *10.45am. Party is in 75 minutes.*

Simone had come out to assess the terrain.

'Here's my two cents,' she said.

'Yes? What do you think? **Help me, Simone**!' I said on the verge of hysterics.

'You break the party into two different vibes,' she said, pacing around like a detective. 'First half, basketball. Loosen people up, break the ice. Then food. People have worked up a hunger by now. We move inside to the living room, where the sound will be easier to control. You do your karaoke in there for the second half of the party, around fourteen-thirty.'

'Yes! That's perfect! That's going to work! Oh, thank you, Simone, you're a lifesaver!'

'No,' she said, like an absolute rockstar. 'I'm a stage manager.'

Then she turned to my dad, who was looking very impressed. 'I'll help you set up the karaoke machine if you like, Mr M. We can hook the bluetooth up to your surround sound.'

'Yeah, great. I've brought a couple of extra mics too, maybe you can help me set them up.'

'Awesome. All g, Mr M,' she said, following Dad inside.

**Party planning: tick.**

Then Mum and I started decorating the outside area with basketball bunting*.

**Outside decorations: tick.**

*Hang on a minute. We have a basketball hoop, but do we have a basket . . .* **ball?**

*If you don't know what bunting is, you are not alone. I was today years old (i.e. thirteen, LOL). Anyway, it's cute little flags on a string, you can google it.

'DAD!' I screamed, running into the living room. 'Did the basketball hoop come with a ball?'

Dad furrowed his brow for what seemed like sixteen business days, then said, 'Ah, now that you mention it, I don't think it did.'

*This is not happening.*

***This is a bad dream.***

*I have a basketball-themed birthday party due to start in* ONE HOUR *and I have* ***no actual basketball.***

I don't know how long I was standing there, paralysed with panic, when Simone said, 'Is anyone coming today who can bring a ball with them?'

I started racking my brain for who might have a basketball at home.

*Of course! Enid said they have a hoop; they must have one at their place!*

'Enid!' I said, ecstatic with relief. 'I'll message her!'

Texts to Enid:

Can you bring a basketball

Forgot to get one LOL

Then, after about thirty-six years, a text finally came back.

LOL LOL LOL

WILL BRING

SEE YOU SOON

**Basketball crisis management: tick.** ☑

Then Dad, Simone and I set up the disco mood lighting in the living room while Mum started getting the snacks ready. We got the final fairy lights up at 11.55am precisely. The room looked totally awesome.

**Karaoke room decorations: tick.** ☑

I was helping Mum put out the chips and dips when we heard the first knock on the door. My heart skipped a beat.

*This is it.*

***It's happening.***

<u>My</u> <u>first</u> <u>teenage</u> <u>birthday</u> <u>party</u>.

'You want to get it, Sugar-puff?' asked Dad.

'Yes! No! I wonder who it is. I'll get it. Should I get it?'

I was coming undone.

'You should definitely get it,' said Simone, smiling. 'It's your party.'

I took a quick, deep breath, then went to open the door.

It was Tyler.

I think my eyes fell out.

He looked so handsome, wearing basketball shorts and vest with the number 13 on it!

*How cute is that?*

'Happy Birthday, Melody Moss,' he said, handing me a present.

'Tyler! Hi! Thank you!' I blurted at him.

I must have been standing there, dumbstruck, for ages, because eventually he had to say, 'Can I come in?'

'Oh, yes! Come in!' He followed me into the living room.

'Am I the first one here?' he asked.

'Yeah. Top marks for punctuality. Boom!' I said.

***BOOM?***

***Really, Melody?***

<u>Get</u> <u>a</u> <u>hold</u> <u>of</u> <u>yourself</u>!

'Tyler, this is my dad. You know Simone.'

'G'day Tyler!' Dad said. 'Loved you in the show last term. You've got quite a voice!' said Dad.

(Poor Dad doesn't know that Tyler was actually miming to Victor singing, but that's another story.)

Knock, Knock, Knock!

''Scuse me,' I said, heading back to the front door.

It was Enid, Rebecca and Connor. They were all dressed in sports gear too.

*People have embraced the theme!*

And Enid was holding a basketball. **Phew!**

'Hi guys! Come in!' I said, showing them to the living room.

'Why don't you hang here until everyone arrives and then you can all head out the back for basketball,' said Mum as she handed out soft drinks.

Knock, Knock, Knock, Knock, Knock, Knock!

I ran to open the door and stop the urgent knocking.

It was Abby. She was wearing a hot-pink tennis skirt and matching top, with a pink plastic visa and sneakers with wedge heels.

'Abby! You look amazing!' She really did.

'Thanks! Happy Birthday!' she said, walking through the door like she's done so many times over the years.

*Here it comes.*

I followed her into the living room, filled with dread.

She saw Tyler.

She stopped in her tracks.

The room went quiet.

Then she put on a smile, looked at my dad and said, 'Hi Mr Moss!'

*I can't believe it. Another crisis averted. Everything is working out perfectly!*

Maud, Zach and the kids from Broadway Babies then turned up and soon everyone was there.

Except Victor.

My heart sank, but I had a party to get on with.

'Let's go play some basketball!' I called out. Everyone cheered and I led them all out the back.

'OMG, Melody it looks so cool out here!' said Enid.

She started bouncing the ball and soon everyone was running around like lunatics, shrieking and having fun. Turns out Simone is really good at basketball. Why am I not surprised? LOL.

Hoop tally:

| | |
|---|---|
| Simone: 5 | Tyler: 2 |
| Connor: 4 | Enid: 1 |
| Rebecca: 3 | Zach: 1 |

No, I did not manage to score a basket, but I had the best time watching all my friends have fun. Connor was really kind, showing people who hadn't played before what to do. He was being especially helpful with Abby.

WAIT.

***WHAT?***

I had to blink a few times to register the image of Connor standing behind Abby the Human Barbie Doll, with his hands over hers holding the ball and helping her shoot it into the hoop. Abby was looking at him like she used to look at Tyler.

*This is my party, for crying out loud! I'm the one who should be having the Big Romantic Moment!*

Then I saw Abby look very pointedly at Tyler while Connor was helping her, and I realised that **she was trying to make Tyler jealous.**

I looked at Tyler as he caught the ball and bounced it a few times.

Tyler was not jealous. Tyler was oblivious.

**LOL LOL LOL LOL LOL**

Soon most of us were exhausted and had to sit down, which is when Mum brought out the food. Chicken katsu, sushi and lots of hot chips with sauce. Yum! And not even that weird! Thanks, Mum ☺

**Basketball half of party: tick.** ☑

When everyone was stuffed, we headed into the living room. Dad had switched all the special lighting on. There were fairy lights and lamps and even a small disco ball. It was like a nightclub! (Not that I've ever been in one, but I've seen them in movies.)

There were bowls of chocolates and lollies, and it was actually really cool to have another activity. It was like having two parties!

The karaoke machine was all set up, with the menu on the TV.

'Who's going first?' I asked.

Everyone went quiet. Nobody said anything. Even Abby, who I thought would be desperate to show off her singing voice.

*Oh no. Nobody wants to sing. The karaoke part of the party is a total flop.*

I was just about to get up and break the ice myself, when music started playing.

*Hang on a minute, I recognise this song . . .*

It was the start of 'Hopelessly Devoted to You' from *Grease*, one of my favourite songs.

*Who's put this on?*

Then I heard a familiar and very beautiful voice start singing. At first I panicked that one of my visitors might have shown up to ruin everything, but when I turned around I saw Victor coming around the corner, holding a microphone and singing!

**OH, VICTOR YOU ABSOLUTE LEGEND OF A FRIEND!!**

I couldn't stop the happy tears rolling down my cheeks.

When he got to the chorus, all the musical-theatre kids joined in and we all shrieked the song out at the top of our lungs.

*Ash would have hated this! Ha ha!*

The ice was well and truly broken and everyone wanted a turn after that.

Karaoke song tally:

| | |
|---|---|
| Victor: 1 | Enid and Rebecca: 1 |
| Abby: 3 | Simone, Maud and Zach: 1 |
| Melody and Victor: 1 | Everyone together: 6! |

By four-thirty, Victor was the only person left. We were sitting on the front verandah, having waved goodbye to the last few friends.

'I didn't think you were going to come,' I said.

'I'm sorry,' he said, smiling. 'I wanted to surprise you, but then Simone texted me that you were doing basketball first, so I had to wait.'

'It was totally worth it,' I replied, giving him a little nudge with my shoulder.

'I'm sorry about how I've been lately,' he said. 'I was really freaked out by what happened in the music room with the little kid.'

'I know. I wish I could stop them. But you know how you said that if we can work out why they come, maybe we can stop it happening?'

'Yeah, I remember,' he said, nodding.

'Well, I was thinking about how you ended up playing the piano and singing "America", and how amazing you were. You're so shy, Victor. Maybe the little kid was trying to bust you out of your shell.'

Victor smiled a little. 'I did feel good after I sang that song,' he admitted. 'But then I freaked out about what people would think of me. Do you think she's going to come back?'

'I don't know. But even if she – or any of them – does, they don't mean any harm. And nobody else can see them but us. Don't ask me why. So, there's nothing to be worried about. Okay?'

'Okay,' he said with a smile. I hoped I'd managed to convince him. I really didn't want to do life without Victor.

Then we went inside to watch the movie of *Cats* and laughed our heads off because it's actually ridiculous.

Mum ordered Thai takeaway because for the first time ever she'd had enough of cooking. Toto was finally let out of my parents' room, where she had been kept prisoner so she didn't snuffle the party food while no-one was looking. I may have slipped her a bit of stir-fried chicken to say sorry.

Today was the absolute best day of my teens so far.

***See what I did there?***

# CHAPTER 21: Teen Swagger

Monday, 19 May
7.12pm

I slept in again this morning! Mum says it's because I'm a teenager now and that's what teenagers do, but I think it's because –

- Yesterday was massive and fabulous and exhausting.
- The lead-up to yesterday was super stressful, so it was Relief Sleep.
- I'd made up with Victor, which made me feel happy and relaxed again.
- It's getting cold now and my bed is super cosy, even if it's full of Toto farts.

When I arrived at school, I really did feel different.

I have gained cool thirteen-year-old status.

*I am rocking up with Teen Swagger.*

I even enjoyed my classes more. Probs because I am older and therefore smarter.

In Art, we had to paint a self-portrait in the style of Picasso*, which was handy because that's the only style I can paint in.

In Maths, we had a multiple-choice test, which is my favourite kind because you don't have to come up with any answers, so I always feel like I nailed it.

*Picasso painted people with their faces all messed up with an eye over here and an ear over there. A bit like how I look when I wake up in the morning. Anyway, google 'Picasso' and you'll see what I mean.

By lunchtime, I was riding high.

*I am a successful teenager, smashing high school.*
*Nothing can get in my way.*

When the lunch bell rang, I almost danced to our spot. I was looking forward to reliving the highlights of yesterday's party with everyone.

I was almost there. I could see Abby, Enid and Epiphany. But . . .

*. . . something's off.*

***None of them are smiling.***

Enid saw me, stood up and came towards me. Strange.

*I have a bad feeling about this.*

'Hi!' I said to her. 'What's up?'

She looked very serious.

'Melody, you better stay away. Abby is really upset with you.'

'What? Why?' I asked.

'Because you invited Tyler to your party. It was really

hard for her yesterday.'

*You have got to be kidding me.*

'But she seemed fine. Everyone had a good time,' I said, confused.

'Well, she was only pretending to be fine because it was your birthday.'

'This is ridiculous! Let me talk to her,' I said. I tried to get around Enid, but she blocked my way.

'You better not, Melody. You promised Abby he wouldn't be there. We all heard you.'

'What, so **everyone's** mad at me?'

*What is even happening right now?*

She shrugged. 'I'm sorry, Melody. Just stay away, okay?'

I looked over to Abby, who looked back at me with **daggers**. Epiphany had a similar expression.

'Fine. Okay. Whatever,' I said and turned away with as much dignity as I could summon, and walked off purposefully to . . .

*Hang on a minute! That's my spot they're sitting in! I've been kicked out of my own actual lunch spot!*

*And where is Victor?*

I didn't know what to do with myself. I had nowhere to sit and no-one to sit with. So, I just wandered around the school until . . .

'Melody!' called a voice.

I looked around and saw Tyler waving to me from the oval.

A friendly face!

'Hi!' I said, walking towards him.

'What are you doing?' he asked. 'Where are the others?'

'Um . . . I think I've been kicked out of the group.'

***Don't cry in front of Tyler!***

'No way! But everyone loves you, Melody Moss. Your party was epic, by the way.'

'Thanks, Tyler, but not everyone agrees with you on that one. Abby is angry that I invited you.'

Tyler frowned, clearly confused.

'But it was **your** party. You should be able to invite whoever you want.'

I shrugged. 'That's what I thought. But I guess she's not over your break-up.'

'She broke up with **me**!' he said, exasperated. 'But . . . to be honest, I was kind of glad.'

He looked a bit guilty but smiled at me like we were both in on the same joke.

'You can have lunch with me, if you like,' he said, sitting on the grass.

'Aren't you playing football?' I asked.

'Nah, not really.'

I sat down next to him.

'Well, I guess we're both kicked out of the group,' he said, with a smile. 'I like it over here anyway. It's quiet.'

So, Tyler and I sat on the edge of the oval and ate our sandwiches together. He had Vegemite, I had cheese and kimchi – one of Mum's specialties and actually delicious, although a little whiffy. We talked about football and basketball, and it wasn't even boring.

*It was really, really, really nice.*

When lunch was over, I said, 'Thanks for letting me hang with you.'

And he said, 'Any time. Seriously. If those Mean Girls won't talk to you tomorrow, come and sit here with me, okay?'

'Okay,' I replied.

*I would rather sit here with you than anywhere in the world, Tyler Francis.*

Later, I passed Abby in the hallway between classes. She completely blanked me. Like I wasn't even there.

Texts with Victor:

where were you today?

SORRY I HAD PIANO EXAM

FORGOT TO TELL YOU

Abby and the others all hate me now

WHY?

Coz Tyler came to my party

THAT'S STUPID

ikr

I DON'T HATE YOU

Thx

Xxx

# CHAPTER 22:
# The Bully

Tuesday, 20 May
6.05am

So, obviously the whole sleeping-in-because-life-is-so-relaxing-and-on-track thing is over. I woke up early **full of dread**.

It's Broadway Babies after school today and half of them aren't talking to me.

Maybe I won't go.

5.34pm

I saw Victor as we were walking into school.

'Hey! Are you coming to Broadway Babies?' I asked.

'Maybe.'

'Please, Victor, you have to!'

'Okay, okay. I just might have a thing I have to do.'

*Why does he look guilty?*

'What thing?' I asked, narrowing my eyes suspiciously.

'It's about my piano exam yesterday. I might have an interview. I'll find out at lunch. I'll text you.' Then he practically ran away from me.

**I do NOT like the sound of that.**

To make things worse, I had two hours of Maths in the morning.

Two hours of pretending to care about the measurements of a triangle.

At one point, I imagined myself standing on my desk and screaming, *I HATE TRIANGLES! EVERYONE HATES TRIANGLES! TRIANGLES ARE BORING! RID THE WORLD OF TRIANGLES!* at the teacher. That would have felt good.

Then I bumped into Epiphany in the hall between classes.

'Hi!' I said.

She looked at me like I'd just squashed her pet mouse with a frypan.

'I can't believe you, Melody.'

*Really? Still? Or have I done some spectacularly terrible new thing?*

'What?' I asked.

'We *saw* you. We saw you with Tyler at lunch yesterday. You obviously invited him to your party because you like him, and now you're moving in on him. Your ex-ex-best-friend's ex-boyfriend!'

*Well, that was confusing.*

I then proceeded to tell several lies:

'I don't like him!'

***Lie number 1.***

'We were just having lunch; it wasn't some romantic thing!'

***Lie number 2.***

'I did *not* invite him because I like him!'

***Lie number 3.***

'Melody, stop lying,' said Epiphany, looking disappointed in me.

'I'm NOT LYING!'

***Lie number 4.***

When the lunch bell rang, I checked my phone sneakily because you're not supposed to use them at school.

Text from Victor:

SORRY I HAVE TO GO TO THIS THING

TALK LATER

*Great. No Victor. No lunch spot.*

*I guess that only gives me one option.*

I made my way to the oval. Tyler was there, kicking his football. He stopped when he saw me and came over.

'Hey Melody Moss. You still in the doghouse?'

'Even worse. We were seen at lunch together yesterday and now I'm some sort of boyfriend-stealer.'

'That's funny,' he said, with a laugh.

*Yes, it probably is. I have about as much chance of 'stealing' Tyler as a fly surviving in a fart factory. And my bedroom often is a fart factory, so I should know.*

'I know, ha-ha.' I laughed weakly and sat on the grass. I was in no mood.

He flopped down next to me and said, 'Well, are you?'

'What?'

'Trying to steal me?' he asked.

***HOW***

***THE***

***HELL***

***DO I ANSWER THAT??***

- 'No, I'm not trying to steal you.' Then he'll think I don't like him.
- 'Yes, I am trying to steal you.' Then he'll think I'm a desperate, deluded embarrassment.

'I'm not trying to steal anyone. You're not her boyfriend anymore, right?'

He smiled at me and said, 'Right.'

*Yes! Nailed it.*

Then we sat on the grass and talked about . . . just stuff. Our families. Holidays. A cloud that looked like Mr Splitz.

The bell rang way too soon.

I was in the middle of Mrs Butcher's class about . . . actually, I have no idea what it was about. I didn't listen to a word she said, I was too busy worrying about what to do this afternoon. Should I –

- Go and face the haters?
- Go home and cry into a bowl of afternoon cereal?
- Go to the airport, get on a flight to New York and spend a month watching Broadway shows? (I wish!)

*Hang on a minute! Musical theatre is my thing! I am the OG musical-theatre fan, and I am* not *giving up my thing because of them!*

STUFF

THAT.

So, when the bell rang, I held my head up high and marched over to the music room with **Pride and Purpose**.

A few people were already there. As I walked in, a hush descended over the room, and everyone looked at me very strangely. I sat on the floor next to Maud, **who moved away from me!** Zach was just staring, as if I had an extra head.

'What?' I asked him.

'Is it true?' he said, looking scandalised.

'Is **what** true?'

'Did you steal Abby's boyfriend?'

<u>*Are you*</u>

<u>*CEREAL*</u>*??*

'What? No!'

Then Maud said, 'But everyone saw you with him at lunch yesterday *and* today and you invited him to your party even though you promised Abby you wouldn't.' She paused for a second then continued with great authority. 'Abby says you broke them up.'

*For a quiet girl, she suddenly has a lot to say.*

'Well, that is just silly. I had nothing to do with it!' I was getting really frustrated with the whole thing now. 'He didn't want to be with her anymore because she is a *pain in the bum*!'

Maud went very pale at that moment and was staring behind me towards the doorway.

Icicles crept over my whole body, like in *Frozen*.

I turned around slowly.

Abby and Enid were standing there.

I opened my mouth to say – I don't know what – but I never got the chance because Abby burst into tears. Enid put her arms around her and guided her to a chair, where she dramatically collapsed, sobbing.

Miss Elliot came out of the next room, looking very concerned.

'What on earth has happened? Abby, are you all right?'

Abby looked up at her, with a tear-stained face and, pointing at me, said, 'Miss Elliot, Melody is **BULLYING ME**!' And burst into a fresh round of sobs.

Miss Elliot looked very confused.

'Melody?' she repeated. Then she looked at me and asked, 'Is this true?'

'No!' I protested.

'Well, you *did* say Tyler broke up with her because she's a pain in the bum. And now you're dating him,' said Zach.

'I AM NOT DATING HIM!' I yelled.

'Please lower your voice,' said Miss Elliot sternly.

*No! Not Miss Elliot too! I can't bear it if she hates me now!*

'Did you say that about Abby?' she asked me.

I looked around the room. Everyone was staring daggers at me, especially Abby.

'Well . . . yes. But I was upset, I didn't mean it. Actually, I *did* mean it, but I shouldn't have said it.'

'I'm really surprised at you, Melody,' said Miss Elliot.

*She has never looked at me like this before.*

'I think, under the circumstances, we should cancel the club meeting for today. Melody and Abby, please stay behind for a minute. The rest of you can go.'

'I'll wait for you out the front, Abby,' said Enid.

After everyone had filed out, Miss Elliot closed the door and sat next to Abby.

'Come and sit, please,' she said to me. 'Is there anything you want to say to Abby?'

*How about: 'You're a lying, manipulative little witch and I hope you get food poisoning'?*

'I'm sorry I called you a pain in the bum,' was what I actually said.

Abby looked at me with the best impression of a sad person I've ever seen.

'I can't believe you stole Tyler from me,' she said.

'I DIDN'T!' I yelled. I was beyond frustrated.

'But **everyone** has seen you together.'

'I was just sitting with him because you kicked me out of my own lunch spot!'

'All right, girls, that's enough! All this nonsense about stealing boyfriends is very silly. You're in Year 7, you should be focusing on more important things, like school and friendships. I really hope that by next Tuesday you'll have resolved things so we can resume our club meetings. Otherwise, I'm going to have to rethink Broadway Babies altogether. I can't have people fighting in here. It's not in the spirit of musical theatre.'

*Actually, all this drama is very musical theatre, in my humble opinion.*

I let Abby and Enid walk to the bus stop, while I went to my favourite **Crying Cubicle** in the girls' toilets.

Then I called Dad to come and pick me up.

I told him I'd had a falling out with Abby. He took me for ice-cream, and we sat in the park.

'I called her a pain in the bum,' I said.

'Well . . . that seems like a pretty accurate description to me,' said Dad with a wink.

He didn't ask me any more questions after that, which was exactly what I needed. We just sat together and that made me feel a tiny bit better.

# CHAPTER 23:
# Fluffy White Poos

Wednesday, 21 May
7.30am

I really really really really really really really don't want to go to school today.

Texts to Victor:

are you going to school

I need back-up

Y

meet you next to the oval at lunch

K

Even over text he is a man of few words.

5.20pm

So, I put on my **Big Girl Pants** and went to school.

Apparently, everyone in Year 7 got the memo that Melody Moss is a **Boyfriend Stealing School Bully** because nobody spoke to me.

Or looked at me.

Or sat with me in class.

It was like I was invisible, but worse, because people don't move away from you when you're invisible. I was like a bad smell. A fart.

**Melody Moss the Human Fart.**

I couldn't wait for lunchtime so I could see Victor and Tyler, the only two people who still seemed to like me. I can't believe my only two friends now are boys. I would like to issue a formal apology to all boys for previously thinking you were all Smelly, Dumb, Gross and Of No Useful Purpose.

I unreservedly withdraw my remarks.

I found Tyler at the oval, sitting in our new spot. I was so happy to see him. But when he saw me approaching, he stood up and walked over. He did not look happy.

'Did you tell Abby I broke up with her because she's a pain in the bum?' he asked.

*Oh no! Not Tyler too!*

'Well . . . yes. Yes, I did.'

'I never said that, Melody.' He seemed so disappointed in me.

'I know. That was more my **interpretation** of what you said. I'm sorry.'

'Why is everyone saying we're going out? Is that what you've been telling people?'

'NO!' I reacted way too strongly. 'Of course not! I'd never say that! That'd be ridiculous! Stupid!

Us going out? Ha! AS IF!'

*Shut up, Melody!*

But the words were already out there, floating around in front of Tyler's face and I couldn't shove them back in my mouth again. He looked kind of hurt.

'Yeah,' he said, nodding sadly. 'As if.'

And then he walked away.

I sat down on the grass and stared at the clouds. None of them looked like Mr Splitz today. More like a bunch of fluffy white poos.

'Hi!' said Victor, plonking down on the grass next to me. 'You look like someone ate all your Easter eggs.'

I was so happy to see him, I nearly burst into tears.

'Oh Victor! I've made such a mess of everything. Even Tyler hates me now!'

'Well, like I said – you do seem to create chaos.'

Then he shared his sandwich with me because Mum had packed me a really weird salad with avocado and banana and I couldn't even with it.

The afternoon was more of the same. Maths, English. Human Fart, etc.

I couldn't wait to get home.

Now I'm in my room listening to *Wicked*, because it's sad and funny and I feel like the characters are my only friends left in the world, apart from Victor.

9.32pm

So, I was sitting on my bed with Toto, listening to 'Loathing', which is a song about really hating someone and sums up how I feel about Abby right now, when I heard a strange scratching sound. I opened my curtains and found myself staring at an

old woman with a kind face, dressed in rags.
I opened the window.

'Well, dear?' she said. 'Aren't you going to let me in? It's freezing out here!'

'It's twenty-two degrees,' I said.

'Well, I'm skin and bones, so I feel it.'

'Who are you?' I asked her.

'Questions, questions! Let's just say I'm a Mysterious Stranger. Now, open up.'

I helped her through the window, which didn't seem like a very practical way for an old lady to come in, but she seemed determined.

Toto was having none of it and scurried under the bed.

The Mysterious Stranger looked deep into my soul.

'You seem like a girl with a problem.'

'You don't know the half of it,' I replied with a sigh.

'No. I know the whole of it,' she said smugly.

'Is that because you're mysterious and wise?'

'No, I read your diary.'

*The sneaky old stickybeak!*

'You can't do that, it's an invasion of privacy!'

She looked completely unbothered.

'Do you want my help, or not?'

'You can't help me. No-one can. *My life is over.*'

I flung myself on the bed.

'That's very dramatic for someone so young. You haven't given up, have you?'

'What else can I do?' I asked, sitting up.

She looked at me for a moment and with a steely eye she said, 'Fight.'

'But how? I made the mess, I said the stupid things. It's all true, what they're saying. I *do* like Tyler, and I *did* call Abby a pain in the bum!'

'That's because she is,' she said with a shrug. 'But the truth isn't always appropriate, which is something you're learning.'

'How can I fix it, then?'

She hit me again with the uncomfortably strong eye contact.

'Lie.'

'But lying is wrong!' I said, standing up. 'What kind of wise old woman *are* you?'

'White lies, dear – do you know what they are?'

She raised a bushy eyebrow.

'Lies that you tell to avoid hurting someone's feelings?' I offered.

'Exactly,' she said with a smile.

'Like telling Mum that dinner was delicious when it wasn't?'

'Yes!' she nodded.

'Or saying someone's haircut suits them when it doesn't?'

'That's it.' She gave a little clap.

'Or telling someone they don't look really old and dirty when they kind of do . . .'

'All right, all right, we get the picture.'

'So . . . I should tell Abby that she's *not* a pain in the bum?' I asked.

'You need to make a full apology. It'll be hard, because we both know that the things she said about you aren't true. But sometimes the only way to fight lies is with more lies.'

*This sounds like really dodgy advice to give a kid, but I'm going to go with it.*

'What about Tyler?'

'That's romance – not my department. I just handle questions of morals, etcetera.'

I didn't realise my visitors were so specialised.

'Okay, right. Well, thanks. I think.'

Then she looked at me, wide eyed, with a sad and innocent little pleading smile.

'Can you spare a few bucks for an old woman?'

'Um, I don't have any cash.'

'No worries, you can tap.'

And then she pulled a little electronic pay machine out of her bra.

I gave her five dollars using my phone and when it pinged, she disappeared!

I think I need to get more sleep.

# CHAPTER 24: The Plan

Thursday, 22 May
8.30am

I can't face school today. I told Mum I'm sick. She didn't seem to mind. I think she can sense I'm in **Teen Crisis**.

I'm going to spend the day planning how to restore my reputation.

12.25pm

Okay, this is the plan:

- Apologise to Abby even though she's been awful to me.

That's as far as I've got.

I really don't want to apologise to Abby, but I have to suck it up.

I'm going back to bed.

Blerg.

# CHAPTER 25: Lies

Friday, 23 May
6.30am

Honestly, my **Big Girl Pants** are getting a workout this term.

I'm going to do it.

Suck it up.

**Apologise.**

Restore my reputation.

9.24pm

Do you know what's not fun?

Well obviously, lots of things, like bending your fingernail back, or getting your dress sucked into an escalator, but specifically to me –

Having everyone in the whole school hate you, that's what's not.

I sat down at my homeroom desk to discover that some brilliant person had written on it. Actually, several people, by the look of the different handwriting.

It said:

Lock up your boy freinds!

BULLYING is rong!

Go and wach a musical LOL

Melody Moss is MEAN.

I looked up to see who had written it, but everyone looked equally happy with themselves.

The spelling mistakes were particularly offensive, so I corrected them with my red Sharpie.

At lunchtime, I went to our spot. Abby was there, with Enid and Epiphany – Zach and Maud too. The **Melody Moss Haters Club** was expanding its membership. Maybe there's a refer-a-friend discount.

I stood there, looking down at them all, trying to summon up my courage.

'Abby doesn't want to talk to you,' said Enid.

Abby didn't look up.

'I know,' I said. 'I just want to apologise.'

She still didn't look up, but nobody was stopping me, so I kept going. It was the biggest load of lies, served up on a plate with fries on the side.
Lie-fries.

List of lies:

- I'm really, really, sorry about what I said.
- You are not a pain in the bum.
- I just said that out of frustration, I didn't mean it.
- Tyler never said anything bad about you.
- I don't like Tyler.
- I never wanted to go out with him.
- Your friendship means more to me than anything.

The last one made her look up. All eyes were on her like she was some kind of Roman Emperor, and I was a gladiator she might throw to the lions to be horrifically torn to shreds.

Then she said, 'Okay.'

'Okay?' I asked. 'You forgive me?'

'Yes, I forgive you,' she said with Great Dignity. 'But I'm very hurt, Melody, so it might take some time till I feel like being your friend again. I just need some space for a while.'

*Win-win, I say.*

And then I did a little bow. Do not ask me why. I was just feeling it. A couple of them looked a bit confused, but Abby seemed happy with it.

I have never been so glad to walk out of school as I was today. I practically ran out of there. I took the shortcut through the basketball court and who should I run into but Connor, shooting hoops.

'Melody! Hi!' he called out when he saw me. I realised that he didn't know about any of it. I guess Year 8 didn't get the memo.

'Hi Connor,' I said. I was so happy to see his warm and cheerful smile.

'You didn't come to basketball club yesterday.'

***That's right!***

'Oh my goodness, I completely forgot. I was sick, anyway. It's been a week!'

My face must have given away more than I meant it to, because he stopped bouncing the ball and walked over to me.

'Is everything okay? You look upset.'

*Stupid face.*

I tried to make light of it.

'Oh, yeah. I was just cancelled for a couple of days because I said some stuff I shouldn't've. But I managed to get out of it alive. Just.'

Connor laughed. 'You're so funny, Melody.'

*That's the nicest thing anyone's said to me all week.*

'You want to shoot some hoops?' he asked with a raised eyebrow.

*Who am I to say no to a tall, handsome, kind Year 8 boy with a basketball in his hands?*

'Sure, why not? I was about to run home and eat

my body weight in Nutella toast, but basketball works, too.'

Connor laughed again.

*I love making him laugh.*

Then he showed me again how to shoot hoops. I tried and failed so many times, but we just laughed and soon I had forgotten about all the awful things that had happened this week.

'Come on, let me help you! I know you can do it!' he said.

Then he stood behind me with his hands over mine while I held the ball, like he had with Abby at my party when Tyler wasn't even watching.

Well, turns out that today . . .

Tyler *was* watching.

Just as I was enjoying the feeling of Connor's big, cool hands covering my little pink pudgy ones, I looked up and saw Tyler walking past the basketball court. He saw Connor and me, then quickly looked away.

Then Connor and I threw the ball together and it went right through the basket.

**Bullseye!**

**My first ever basket!** I screamed with excitement and Connor high-fived me.

'Now you're definitely ready for basketball club!' he said.

'Thanks, Connor, that was so fun!'

'Always fun spending time with you, Melody Moss.'

*I kid you not, he actually said that.*

I think my face turned roughly the colour of Ronald McDonald's hair.

'Well, I'll see you around,' I said, grabbing my bag.

'I'll walk with,' he said, grabbing his.

Then we walked to the bus stop and caught the bus together and I sat right next to him, and the outside of his leg brushed the outside of my leg and now I can never wash that leg again, which is going to make showering really difficult. But worth it.

# CHAPTER 26: Funny Haha

Saturday, 24 May
9.00am

Thinking about Connor.

10.14am

Wonder if he's thinking about me.

12.55pm

If someone thinks *you're* funny, does that mean they *like* you, like you?

1.27pm

Maybe he just thinks I'm funny like a monkey riding a bicycle.*

Or a teacher falling over.

Or Jack Black.

Not Funny and Attractive. Just Funny haha.

*This is well worth your Google time.

3.45pm

Maybe Funny haha is better than nothing.

5.30pm

**I WANT TO BE FUNNY AND ATTRACTIVE!**

# CHAPTER 27: Happy Memories

Monday, 26 May
7.45pm

Today started off better.

I decided to move desks in my homeroom so I don't have to look at the misspelled personal criticisms.

People weren't giving me as many greasy looks like Friday. Maybe a new memo went out un-cancelling me.

We had a relief teacher in Science who let us do whatever we wanted, so I put my earbuds in and listened to the Original Broadway Cast Recording of

*Chicago*. It's about these two girls who have a love/ hate relationship and . . . Now I think about it, that seems to be a thing.

At lunch, I met Victor outside the school hall. I couldn't face the others just yet. Or perhaps ever. And I certainly didn't want to go anywhere near Tyler, who I'm pretty sure hates me now. It was unlocked, so we snuck in.

I felt at home here because we had rehearsed and performed our show there last term, so I had Happy Memories. But . . .

Victor was acting strange, even for him.

He was extremely quiet, even for him.

He was avoiding eye contact, even for him.

We sat in the back seats, in the big empty hall, which smelled like old wood and dust.

'Come on,' I said, 'out with it.'

'Out with what?' he asked, looking guilty as hell. Victor is a terrible actor.

'What have you done?'

He stopped eating his sandwich and put it back in his lunchbox.

Silence.

'What is it, Victor? You're giving me the willies,' I said.

'The what?' he asked, slightly horrified.

'I don't know, it's something my mum says. What's going on?'

He just stared at the rejected sandwich.

'I'm sure it's not as bad as you think,' I offered. 'Did you poo your pants?' I joked.

'No!'

'Did you . . . break an expensive Apple product?'

'No.'

'Did you . . . fall in love with Abby?'

'Yuck, NO!'

'Have you stolen something, got arrested, lied to the police and framed an innocent man for your crime –'

'I'M MOVING SCHOOLS!' he blurted out.

***Oh.***

***That is worse than anything I could have imagined.***

For once in my life, I was speechless.

Victor looked at me with tears in his eyes.

'You know that piano exam I did? It was for the Conservatorium High School. It's a special music school. Then I had an interview for it. I got in, Melody.'

*Don't cry don't cry don't cry.*

'That's . . . amazing, Victor. Congratulations! I'm so happy for you.'

'You don't have to say that,' he said with a small smile.

'I mean it. You're *so* good. You deserve to go there. You're wasted here!'

'I didn't know how to tell you, and then there was all the drama with Abby and . . .' He broke off, clearly upset.

I was upset too, but I didn't want him to see it.

'When do you leave?' I asked.

'At the end of term,' he said sadly.

***Only a few weeks away!***

'But you're happy about it, right?' I asked.

'I'm happy I got in, but I'm not happy that I'm not going to see you every day anymore. I've never had a friend like you.'

'Something tells me the music school will be full of People Like Us. I bet you make lots of friends there.'

'But Melody, how on earth will you cope without me?' he asked, then laughed.

'I WILL PROBABLY DIE!' I shrieked.

And we sat there, laughing and crying and feeling lots of Big Feelings.

But seriously, I probably will die. ☹

# CHAPTER 28: Strong Independent Woman

Tuesday, 27 May
7.46am

Victor's news has made everything else feel a lot less important. All the business with Abby and Tyler, being cancelled, even Connor, pales in comparison to this huge and life-changing turn of events. Victor has been my saviour in high school and now he's leaving after only half a year. I must find a way of coping without him.

I must become a **Strong Independent Woman**.

After some research on the World Wide Web, I've figured out what I'll need to achieve this:

- A Power Suit. Some big shoulder pads in my school blazer should do it.
- A commanding voice. I'm going to speak in a Very Low Voice like Cate Blanchett because she is a Very Serious Actor.
- Strong eye contact with anyone I'm talking to. This will make me intimidating, so people respect me.
- A confident stride. I've been practising walking up and down the hall, taking longer paces and swinging my arms more vigorously.

I'm going to try all of this at school today and see if it makes me feel like a Strong Independent Woman.

6.44pm

I strode through the school gates, taking very long paces and swinging my arms vigorously. It seemed to be working. I did feel more powerful, and I got quite a few looks from people who were probably intimidated by my confidence.

In English, Mrs Bing asked me a question about syntax and I answered in a Very Low Voice*, which caught her off guard. She didn't say anything, but I think she was surprised by how smart I seemed.

*BTW it is hard not to frown when you're talking in a Very low Voice. Try it.

Victor and I decided that the hall was our new hang at lunchtime. When I met him there, I strode up purposefully and looked right into his eyeballs and said in a Very Low Voice, 'Good afternoon, Victor, shall we partake of our lunch in the hall again this fine Tuesday?'

'What's wrong with you?' he asked. 'You sound like Darth Vader.'

'I'm a Strong Independent Woman, Victor.'

'Why are you walking like a robot?'

'It's my confident stride!'

I showed him again, to help him understand. He didn't look impressed.

'Have you been doing this all day?'

'Yes, and I feel very powerful, actually,' I said in my Very Low Voice, staring into his eyes.

'Well, you look ridiculous. Stop it.'

And so that was the end of that.

So much for being a Strong Independent Woman.

We ate our lunch in the back of the hall again, which was probably the quietest place in the whole school.

'You know what this afternoon is?' I asked.

'Tuesday?'

'Broadway Babies.'

He winced.

'I don't know, Melody. I only have a few weeks left here. There doesn't seem much point in me going.'

'I just need you to be my wingman until I'm back in the good books with everyone.' And then I said, 'Please, Victor,' with my special Very Low Voice and unwavering eye contact.

'Okay, okay, just stop talking like that, you're freaking me out.'

So, after school, I went to the music room to face the – well, music.

I was the first one there. Despite Victor's disapproval, I was still enjoying my new purposeful walk, and it gets me places fast.

Miss Elliot was sitting at the piano, making notes on some music. I had been feeling really worried that she might not like me anymore, after she saw me at my worst last week, and I was hoping to apologise. When she saw me, she smiled and said, 'Ah, Melody, I'm glad you're here first. I've been meaning to check in with you. Has everything settled down now with you and Abby?'

'Yes,' I replied. 'I told her I was really sorry for what

I said, and she said she forgives me.'

'That's great. It's hard to say sorry sometimes, especially when we're feeling hurt. But I'm glad you were able to be the bigger person.'

'I also wanted to apologise to you, Miss Elliot, for my behaviour. It's no excuse, but I have been having a bit of a stressful time at school lately.'

'Thank you, Melody, I appreciate that. I know you're a good person, which is why I was surprised that you acted so out of character.'

'I guess I was just having a really bad day. I'm sorry.'

She smiled at me so kindly, that everything felt better again.

When Abby and Enid arrived, they even said hello to me! I'm sure it was partly for Miss Elliot's benefit, but at least we were all on speaking terms again.

'Okay, gang,' said Miss Elliot, once everyone was there. 'I'm glad we could all resolve our differences and get on with the very serious business of musical-theatre appreciation. As no-one has selected a show to focus on today, I've decided that we should listen to *Wicked*. And I have a surprise for you all. At the end of term, I'm going to take you all to see *Wicked* live on stage.'

*OH MY GOD OH MY GOD OH MY GOD OH MY GOD*

Everyone went berserk. People were crying, hugging each other, jumping up and down. Miss Elliot copped a few hugs as well. She was laughing at how excited we all were.

'I'll send an email out to your parents, with a special school discount. And, I have another surprise . . .'

***I don't think my little heart can take any more!***

'Not many people know this, but I actually used to do a bit of performing. I happen to know a couple of the current cast of *Wicked*, and they're going to let us backstage to meet them.'

That's it.

***I'm dead.***

I'm officially deceased.

We spent the rest of the class listening to *Wicked* and singing along at the top of our lungs because of course we know all the words.

I was striding to the bus stop – long strides, arms swinging – when Enid caught up with me.

'Hey Melody! Gee, you walk fast! I just wanted to say that it was really good that you apologised to Abby.'

'Thanks, Enid. You know, I was never trying to steal Tyler away from her.'

She looked confused for a moment. 'Then why were you having lunch with him?'

'Because we're friends, I guess, and I didn't think it was wrong. Was it wrong?'

'Abby seems to think so.'

We'd arrived at the bus stop and I turned to face her.

'Enid, do you think Abby is always right about everything?' I asked.

'I guess,' she replied, looking thoughtful. 'I mean, Rebecca is mostly right about everything, so I probably just expect people to be. But I'm glad you guys aren't fighting anymore.'

Some people are leaders and some people are followers. Enid is definitely a follower.

'Are you coming to basketball club on Thursday?' she asked as the bus pulled up.

*A chance to spend time with Connor, are you kidding?*

'Yeah, probably,' I said, trying to sound casual. 'Could be fun.'

Can't wait.

# CHAPTER 29: New Favourite Hobby

Wednesday, 28 May
7.12pm

Passed Connor in the hall today.

I did an old-fashioned curtsy and said, 'Top of the morning to you!' and made him laugh, which is my new favourite hobby.

'See you at basketball tomorrow?' he asked.

'Oh, tomorrow, is it?' I said, like I'd forgotten. 'Yes, I think I can make it.'

*i.e. I am counting down the seconds until I get to spend time with/near/anywhere around you.*

# CHAPTER 30: Looking Athletic

Thursday, 29 May
6.32pm

I am now at least two years older after getting though today's classes.

Tallest mountain in the world? Sooo not interested.

The themes in *Pride and Prejudice*? Don't care.

The difference between an acute and an isosceles triangle? Actively don't want to know.

*All I care about is getting to that basketball court at precisely 3.05pm!*

At lunchtime, Victor and I ate at the back of the hall again. We like the cool and quiet of our new secret spot. I carefully opened my lunch because it smelled kind of funky.

'Excuse me, you shouldn't be in here! Explain yourself this instant!' yelled a voice from behind, which scared the hell out of us, but when we turned around, it was just Simone the Stage Manager, who started laughing her head off.

'You should've seen your faces!' she said, doubling over.

We both joined in laughing with her until she said, 'But, seriously, guys, I am going to have to ask you to leave. You're getting crumbs everywhere.'

So, Victor and I were homeless again.

'You know what? This is ridiculous!' I announced. 'WE found that spot behind the Science Building, WE should be sitting there!'

'I can't tell you how much I don't want to sit with those girls,' said Victor, making a face.

'We don't have to sit *with* them. We can sit *near* them. Come on.'

So, we went to our spot and casually sat down about three metres away from where Abby, Enid, Epiphany, Maud and Zach were sitting.

They all looked a bit confused by this bold move.

'Hi!' I called out to them cheerfully, and a couple of them tentatively waved back.

We are now officially a splinter group.*

*Not a support group for people with splinters, in case you were wondering, although I think this could catch on, because those things are traumatising.

When the bell rang at the end of the day, I stood up so fast I got a little head spin, which made running impossible, so I walked as fast as I safely could to the basketball court.

I was the first one there, so I put down my bag and decided to do some stretching, so as to look athletic. Thing is, I don't really know how to do stretching, having not been a sporty type of person up until now.

I took a hold of my foot and tried to pull it up in front of me, which is really hard, but I'm sure I saw someone do it once. I managed to get a grip on it, but just as I thought, *Yes, I am nailing this stretch!* I lost my balance.

I was, therefore, flat on my back with my legs in the air, like a dying cockroach, when Connor arrived.

'Um . . . are you okay?' he asked.

*Why am I always flailing on the ground in front of him?!*

'Oh yeah, just napping. Love a pre-game nap,' I joked.

This, of course, made him laugh. Enid and Rebecca rocked up soon, and then six more Year 8 kids who were all very tall and sporty looking. I was feeling quite inadequate, but Connor was very kind.

'Guys, this is Melody and Enid. They're only just learning to play, so let's help them with their technique and just have a friendly muck-around kind of game today.'

Then we split into teams. I was in Connor's and Enid was in Rebecca's. I basically didn't do anything useful to help my team, but I tried to look busy.

A tall, redheaded girl called Cassie won most of the other team's baskets. I was watching her, kind of amazed. Like she was a tropical fruit you've never seen before. Or a rare fungus.

Their team got four baskets, and our team got five! Mostly scored by Connor. I just stood around waving my arms in the air, which seems to be the main thing you do in basketball. That and yell at people to throw the ball to you.

At the end, we were all puffed and thirstily drinking the dregs of our water bottles. Connor always looks particularly good at this time of the day because of the way the sun lights up his hair. It's an excellent time to gaze upon him.

I was right in the middle of gazing, when Connor caught me! But he cracked a smile and said, 'You did good, Melody! Did you have fun?'

Pretty sure I blushed. My heart definitely did a small somersault.

'I did!' I replied. 'I don't really know what I'm doing, though. I think I might need another coaching session. I feel a bit like one of those inflatable things outside a car yard.'

I waved my arms around to demonstrate. This really cracked him up.

'You are hilarious, seriously! Hey Cassie, come and meet Melody!'

*I'm sorry, what was that now?*

The tall, redheaded sporty girl came over and *put her arm around Connor*.

MY CONNOR.

'Cassie, this is Melody, she is deadset the funniest person! Melody, this is my girlfriend, Cassie.'

***Girlfriend.***

***Of course.***

What was I thinking?

'Hi!' she said, all warm and bubbly.

*Go slam your face in a car door.*

*Melody! That is super violent and inappropriate, get a hold of yourself!*

'Hi!' I said with my best, most convincing, friendliest smile.

Then I had to make **Small Talk** with them both all the way to the bus stop and on the bus home.

I've never felt more ridiculous in my life.

And that's saying something, because I invented feeling ridiculous.

There is not enough Vegemite toast in the world for this.

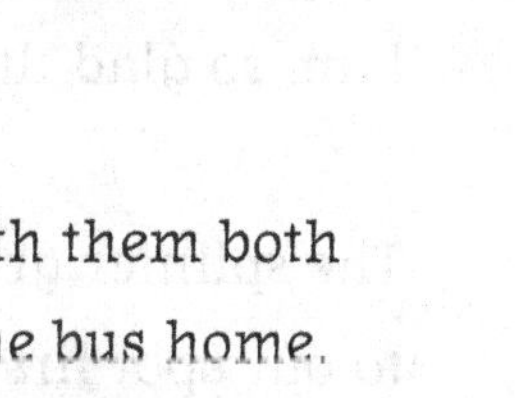

# CHAPTER 31: Lime Juice and Tears

Friday, 30 May
9.39pm

I am so glad this week is over.

The splinter group didn't last long. Victor and I got to our spot first today, which made it awks for Enid when she arrived, so she just sat with us, and so did everyone else.

Somehow, order has been restored to the lunch spot. The only person missing now is Tyler. I wonder if he is still mad at me.

Dad came over for dinner tonight, which is kind of a Friday thing. Mum really outdid herself. She's still in her Mexican phase and made a thing with lots of raw fish and lime juice, which I was actually living for.

Ash, not so much.

'Can you please cook mine?' she said, looking at it, horrified.

'It's ceviche*,' said Mum. As though that explained everything.

(*pronounced ser-vee-chay)

Ash just looked at her blankly.

'It's cooked by the lime juice,' Mum added cheerfully.

'It's not though, is it? It's still raw,' said Ash, poking it.

'You eat raw fish on sushi,' said Dad helpfully.

'That's different. It's **Japanese**.' She stood up. 'I'm gonna cook it.'

So, she went and put her plate in the microwave. I don't know much about cooking, but it didn't seem like a very good idea to me.

'I got an email from Miss Elliot today about the excursion to see *Wicked*. That's very exciting!' said Mum.

'Yes,' I said flatly.

'What's the matter, Babycakes?' asked Dad.

I couldn't hold it in any longer and sighed miserably.

'Victor is leaving to go to the Conservatorium High School.'

Mum and Dad shared a look, which I knew from experience meant that they understood the gravity of the news but there was nothing they could do to make it better. You know. That look.

'That's very exciting for Victor,' said Dad.

'But a bit sad for you, darling,' said Mum.

And then I burst into tears.

'I don't know what to do without him, he's my best friend!' I sobbed.

Dad gave me one of his best cuddles and I cried and cried.

Then Ash came back with her plate of nuked fish. She took one bite and spat it out. 'It's even *worse* now!' she wailed.

'Could've told you that,' said Mum, having none of it.

Then I ate my ceviche, which was now cooked by both lime juice and tears.

**TGIF ☹**

# CHAPTER 32: Growth Spurt

Sunday, 1 June
10.30am

OMG.

**Guys.**

**It's happening.**

My growth spurt.

I was just in the kitchen getting my muesli and standing next to Ash at the counter when Mum walked in and stared at us for a moment.

'What?' said Ash.

'Stand back-to-back,' said Mum.

Ash looked annoyed but we did it anyway.

'Melody, you're nearly as tall as Ash! When did that happen?'

When **did** that happen?

Maybe while I was having my heart broken by Connor, or by Tyler, or I was getting cancelled for bullying Abby or trying to learn basketball. I mean, it's been a busy term.

'I think you're going to be taller than all of us,' said Mum, pouring herself a cup of tea.

Ash looked absolutely furious and walked out of the kitchen without saying anything.

I can't wait to look down on her, hee hee. ☺

# CHAPTER 33: Nose Levels

Monday, 2 June
7.34pm

Realising that I'm taller has given me a bit of a boost.

I'm no longer the little twelve-year-old who walked into high school six months ago!

I've become a bit obsessed with seeing who I am taller than.

Victor, definitely. Maud, for sure.

But the best one?

Abby.

***I am now taller than Abby!***

It wasn't easy to discover this information. I got to our spot early at lunchtime and instead of sitting down, I stood there, pretending to look at a nearby tree. Then when Abby arrived, I stood as close as I could to her without arousing suspicion. I could tell I was a bit taller than her because of where our noses were. So, unless the top of her head is abnormally long, I am definitely the winner. Not that it's a competition. But it is nice not to be the shortest anymore.

The other surprising thing that happened today was that Abby and Zach were holding hands!

*I did not see that one coming.*

Zach looked very happy with himself. Like he'd won a prize in a claw machine. Or found an extra M&M in the bottom of a presumed-empty packet.

When the lunch bell rang, I stood up quickly to see who else I was taller than.

Not Enid – she and her sister are super tall.

Maybe Epiphany. I cornered her before she walked away. I had to get our faces abnormally close to figure it out. She kept moving back because it was probably weird and a lot, but I **needed to know**.

I tried to keep her talking so she wouldn't suspect what I was up to.

'Hey, are Abby and Zach a thing now?' I asked her.

*Assessing nose levels.*

'Yeah, he asked her out on Friday,' she said, backing away slightly.

'I guess she's over Tyler, then,' I said.

*Moving closer.*

'I guess so. She and Zach have more in common, anyway. Zach loves musicals and singing and stuff.'

*Yes, her nose is definitely below mine.*

'Anyway . . . I better . . . get to class,' she said, backing away.

I think she was glad to get away from me being all up in her grill.

After school, I saw Tyler walking out through the gates. I gave him a little smile and he gave me a little smile back!

Maybe he has forgiven me.

# CHAPTER 34: clouds

Tuesday, 3 June
6.12am

I have decided to be a **Very Brave Girl** and actually talk to Tyler. I feel bad that he isn't in our group anymore. Maybe now that Abby is dating Zach, she won't mind if Tyler hangs with us again.

**#gettylerbackinthegroup**

has officially launched.

## 7.00pm

I saw Tyler in the stairwell between classes and I smiled at him properly this time.

'Hi Tyler,' I said.

'Hi,' he said back.

*Excellent progress.*

At lunchtime, I made my move. Of course, I knew exactly where to find him.

He was sitting on the side of the oval, where we had eaten lunch together. I walked up behind him. I didn't want him to see me approaching and get frightened off, so I decided that an ambush was the best strategy.

'That one looks like a kangaroo,' I said.

He turned around to see me pointing to a cloud, which actually did look like a kangaroo, but not for long because they change very quickly. Luckily, he saw it in time.

'It does,' he agreed. 'But now it looks like Santa.'

'And now it looks like a frog,' I said. I sat down next to him, and we continued naming cloud shapes.

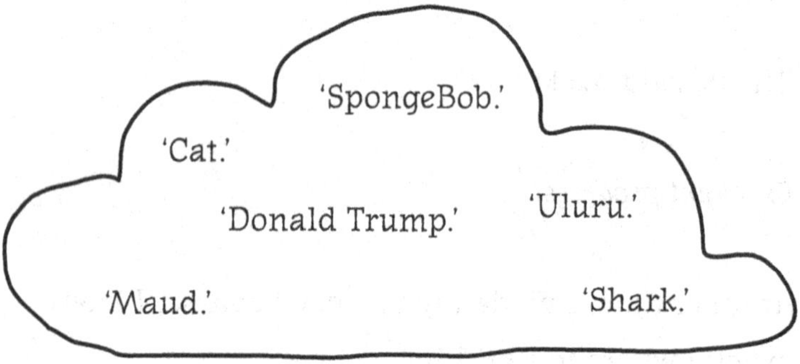


'Tyler,' I said after we had run out of clouds, 'I'm really sorry that I told Abby you thought she was a pain in the bum.'

'It's okay,' he said with a little smile.

**Phew.**

Encouraged by this, I went on. 'It's not the same without you at lunch. Will you come back and sit with us?'

He looked out at the oval. 'I think Abby kind of hates me right now.'

'I don't think so. I think she's over it. Anyway, she's going out with Zach now.'

Tyler's eyes lit up. 'She is?'

'Yeah, so you're off the hook!' I said, nudging him.

He looked pretty relieved about this.

'So, come on,' I said, standing up. 'Let's go over there. You can't be a **Nigel Nofriends** forever.'

He laughed at that.

'Okay, okay!' he said, getting up.

As we were walking, he said, 'You were right, you know.'

'About what?' I asked.

'Abby. She *is* a pain in the bum.'

He smiled the cheekiest smile.

Then we both cracked up.

When we got to our spot, I could sense that he was nervous, but it ended up being totally fine. Nobody batted an eye. Abby's eyes were too busy gazing lovingly at Zach.

PDA* alert!

*Public Display of Affection (vom)

'Hi Tyler,' said Victor, like it was just an ordinary day.

Victor is the best.

**#gettylerbackinthegroup** successful!

We had Broadway Babies after school. Abby and Zach had prepared the duet 'As Long as You're Mine' from *Wicked*. They were actually pretty good, in a nauseating kind of way. Victor made a sneaky gag face at me during it, and it was very, very hard not to laugh.

***Two weeks till* Wicked*!!!***

# CHAPTER 35: PDAs

Thursday, 5 June
7.30am

I am totally dreading basketball club this afternoon.

Now that I know Connor has a tall, athletic, redheaded girlfriend, joining basketball club seems a lot less appealing. But after telling *everyone* that I'm expanding my interests, I can't give up after only going once.

## 5.30pm

Tyler sat with us at lunch, and it felt like everything was back to normal. Except for the weird Abby/Zach PDAs, which were *a lot.*

Abby/Zach PDAs included:

- Earlobe stroking. Just weird.
- Calling each other 'Boo'. Ridiculous.
- Tying and untying each other's shoelaces. Um, why?

Victor and I couldn't look at each other.

When I got to the basketball court after school, Connor and Cassie were there, holding hands.

*Must I be surrounded by gooey, loved-up couples everywhere I turn?*

What made it even worse was that they were both so stupidly warm and friendly to me.

*How am I supposed to hate them when they are so flipping* **NICE**?

I must admit, not being so invested in Connor did help me concentrate on the actual game of basketball.

I think I'm getting better!

Maybe it's the extra height.

# CHAPTER 36: Slaying

Friday, 6 June
4.46pm

So . . .

I was fleeing school at the end of the day because I'd had enough of everyone's nonsense and I couldn't get home to my toaster fast enough, when I bumped into Tyler. We walked together to the bus stop, just chatting about schoolwork we had to do and boring stuff like that when OUT OF NOWHERE, he looked at me and said, 'Do you want to hang out on the weekend?'

***Well, cover me in breadcrumbs and bake me for fourteen minutes!***

Look casual!

Look normal!

**Look un-interested!**

'Um . . . yeah, sure,' I said vaguely.

'You could come to my house, but Billy will be there and he's a bit of a handful . . .'

'Yes, I know!' (Having babysat Billy last term, I know he is more than a handful. He is an actual terrorist.)

'You could . . . come to my house, if you like?' I offered casually. 'I promise I won't make you listen to musicals or sing or anything.'

He laughed. 'Okay. Your place is cool. You still got that basketball hoop?'

'As a matter of fact, we do.'

'Awesome, that was fun. I'll see you tomorrow then. Like, three?'

'Great,' I said, trying very, very hard to seem normal. As though this wasn't **the first time in my entire life that a boy has shown any interest in me.**

6.50pm

I have **ransacked** my wardrobe looking for something to wear tomorrow.

I've tried on EVERYTHING and nothing looks right.

What's more – nothing fits!

Stupid growth spurt.

Aaaaaggggghhhhhh!!!!!

8.15pm

After having a Total Breakdown and telling Mum that if I don't look good tomorrow my life is **not worth living**, she said, 'Well, it's too late to go shopping. Maybe Ash might have something that will fit you.'

That was when I knew Mum had officially lost the plot. As if Ash would lend me anything. She literally hates me.

We knocked on her door. I don't see inside Ash's room very often because the door is always closed. It's **neat** in there. Like, obsessively neat. Pens-lined-up-in-order-of-length neat.

'Ash – Melody has a friend coming over tomorrow and none of her clothes seem to fit. Do you have something that might suit her?' asked Mum.

'What kind of friend?' asked Ash, narrowing her eyes.

'A boy,' I replied in a small voice, hideously embarrassed by the whole thing.

She looked at my desperate, tear-stained face and I saw a glimmer of something . . .

*Pity.*

Then she went to her wardrobe and took out a pair of black jeans and a dark pink long-sleeved top.

*Maybe she is human after all.*

'These should fit you,' she said, handing them to me.

And they did. I tried them on in my room and they sit on me just right.

In fact . . .

**I am slaying.**

# CHAPTER 37: So Many Questions

Saturday, 7 June
7.45am

I did not sleep a single, solitary skerrick of a wink!*

I just tossed and turned.

*What is a skerrick, anyway? A tadpole? A small ferret? A pirate's ear wax?

**So**

**many**

**questions:**

- Does Tyler really *like* me, like me?
- If so, why me? Why now?
- Will he tell me, or do I have to guess?
- What on earth will we actually do tomorrow? Just talk? Watch TV?
- Is this a date?
- Do I need to send some sort of signal or sign that I like him? Like a wink, or a nod, or just open my eyes really wide and raise my eyebrows? (I just tried this one in the mirror and I don't think it's the go.)

I decided the best thing to do is absolutely nothing. No sudden moves or noises. I don't want to alarm him and scare him off.

12.30pm

I was too nervous to eat anything all morning, then I was suddenly **RAVENOUS** and ate half a barbequed chicken, a heap of cold mashed potato and a punnet of chocolate mousse. Now my stomach looks like an alien is about to burst out of it!

***What have I done?***

2.15pm

I googled 'what to do if you ate too much' and the internet said to go for a walk. I figured if a walk helps, then running must be even more effective, so I ran as fast as I could around the block, tripped over a bit of pavement **that should have been smooth**, fell flat on my face and now my face is bleeding! I have a massive gravel rash on my cheek, and I look like I've been savaged by an angry Chihuahua*!

*Google 'angry Chihuahua' and you'll get the idea. Those things are LIVID.

So, for my first ever date with a boy, I have:

- A huge swollen tummy from overeating.
- A bleeding face.
- Low-level hysteria.

7.20pm

My hysteria was interrupted by Tyler knocking on the door at exactly three o'clock. I took a final deep breath and tried to compose myself before going to let him in.

I opened the door, and he was standing there, smiling, all normal, like he pops round all the time just to hang out with me. He was wearing jeans and a T-shirt, with a check shirt open over the top and he looked **indescribably** handsome. Seriously, I won't even try.

'Hi,' I said. 'Welcome to my humble abode.'

'Why, thank you,' he said, smiling.

And **then** he said, 'You look nice.'

OH, MY SWEET BABY CUCUMBER SALAD!! HE THINKS I LOOK NICE!! IS HE BLIND??

'I fell over,' I said, embarrassed. 'That's why my face looks like this.'

'Can't even notice it,' he said. 'How did you fall over?'

'Oh, you know, just going for a jog.' I did a little sporty jogging move.

*You're overselling it, Melody!*

'Um . . . can I come in?' he finally said.

*Why can't I invite people in like a normal human?*

'Oh, golly-gosh, yes! Sorry! Come in!'

We went out the back and shot some hoops (well, he did) and just chatted. I told him how Victor is leaving at the end of term.

'I don't know what I'm going to do without him,' I said sadly.

'Well, you'll have me,' he said.

*'You'll have me.' I can't believe he said that!*

Then we went inside and said hi to Mum, who gave us lemonade and chips to take to the front verandah.

We sat on the verandah chairs looking out at the street and I had no idea what to do next.

*Tyler is on my verandah.*

Then he looked at me, kind of seriously, but also smiling. Seriously smiling.

'So, um, Melody . . .'

*Yes?*

'I just wanted to say . . .'

**Yes?**

'That, ah . . . I really, ah . . .'

***Yes?***

'I really like you.'

**OH**

**MY**

**CHEESE**

**AND**

**BISCUITS**

***What do I do, what do I do, what do I do?***

Say something, Melody!!

'I really like you too,' I finally managed to get out.

That made him smile and him smiling made me smile.

'I was wondering if you'd like to be my . . . girlfriend?'

***DO NOT VOMIT, MELODY!***

'Um, yes. Yes, I would really like that,' I said, grinning from ear to ear like a fool.

'Okay!' he said.

'Okay!' I said.

Neither of us really knew what to do next, and the eye contact was getting way too intense, so we both looked out at the street for a moment.

Thankfully, he broke the awkwardness.

'Do you want to . . . go for a walk?' he asked.

'Sure!' I said **to my new boyfriend**.

So, we walked to the park and on the way there,

**TYLER**

**HELD**

**MY**

**HAND.**

There I was, walking hand in hand with a boy I like and who likes me, and it was the best feeling I have ever had in my whole entire life to date on this earth full stop.

When we got back, we sat on the verandah again and looked out at the street and talked.

'Do you think we should tell people at school?' I asked him.

'I don't need to make some big announcement. I'm just happy you said yes,' he said, smiling.

'Well, I've actually liked you for a really long time. But you were with Abby and . . .'

*Shut up, Melody, you sound way too keen, be cool, be cool!*

'Well, I thought maybe you liked Connor,' said Tyler. 'Because he was at your party, and then I saw you guys on the basketball court one time, and you looked really happy.'

'Oh, no! He has a girlfriend in Year 8. She's really nice. Connor was never interested in me,' I said.

'Well, he's crazy,' said Tyler, taking my hand, 'because you are one of a kind, Melody Moss.'

He leaned over and kissed me very softly and sweetly on the cheek, like a real gentleman. His lips were so nice and warm on my face, although it did hurt a little bit because of my massive gravel rash, but I didn't mind.

And then I heard the strangest thing . . .

*Applause.*

And cheering . . .

***What the –***

I looked at my bedroom window, and there were faces pressed against the glass, trying to get a look.

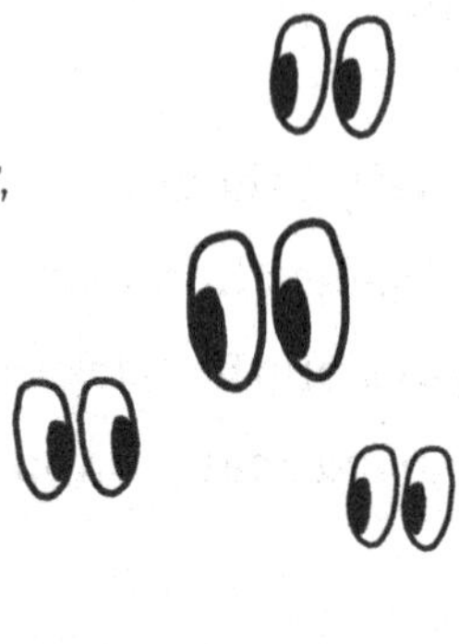

The Revolutionary Soldier.

The Mysterious Stranger.

The Little Girl.

The Mermaid.

The Witch.

Every character that had visited me, and even some that hadn't, were all inside my bedroom looking through the window, cheering and clapping!

Tyler didn't seem to notice, thank goodness. But I couldn't help smiling. I gave them a little wink and they all waved at me.

My very own cheer squad **LOL**.

# CHAPTER 38: Texts with Tyler

Sunday, 8 June
4.00pm

I was super worried about what to do next because I can sometimes be Extra, and I don't want to scare off my first ever boyfriend within 24 hours of obtaining him. Luckily, he texted me first.

Texts with Tyler:

HEY MELODY

SO GLAD YOU SAID YES

X

hey yourself

so glad you asked me

x

MISS YOU ALREADY

XX

me too

cant wait to see you tomorrow

xx

***Sigh.***

# CHAPTER 39:
# A Normal Monday

Monday, 9 June

4.56pm

**Day 2** of having a boyfriend ☺.

I know Tyler said he didn't want to make some big announcement, so I had to respect that. But **the only thing I wanted to do** was make some big announcement.

If I had my way, I would get:

- A sky-writing plane spelling out Melody + Tyler OMG.
- A marching band parading through the school playing non-stop musical-theatre love songs.
- A team of florists to write Melody 4 Tyler in roses across the school lawn.
- A troupe of acrobats to carry Tyler and me through the school gates on their shoulders, with an occasional somersault for good measure.

It was hard not to shout it from the rooftop of the Science Building.

I realised I hadn't even told Victor yet!

Luckily, I found him at our lunch spot before anyone else got there.

'Victor! I have to tell you something!' I said urgently.

'Oh no, what now?' he said, clearly worried.

'Why do you assume it's bad news?'

'Because it usually is with you.'

'Well, this time it's good news!'

I paused for dramatic effect.

'Tyler asked me to be his girlfriend!'

I did a very small squealy happy dance.

Victor looked a bit sad.

'Aren't you happy for me, Victor?' I asked.

He nodded slightly and looked like he might cry.

'I'm really happy for you. You've liked him for ages, and I think he's really cool. I'm just thinking . . . it's perfect. With me going. I don't feel so bad about leaving you alone now.' He gave a little shrug and a smile.

'Oh Victor!' I said, throwing my arms around him. He's not a fan of physical affection, but he took it. 'We are going to be best friends for ever and ever!' I went on. 'Even though we're at different schools, we'll still see each other all the time. Okay?'

'Promise?' he said, looking up at me through his ginormous glasses like a pug.

'Promise,' I said, and we shook hands on it to seal the deal.

The others all rocked up soon, last of all Tyler. We shared a special smile and Victor moved over to let him sit between us. I could see on Victor's face that he really was happy for me.

***Then Tyler put his arm around me.***

It felt so nice, and so **exciting** for him to do that in front of everyone.

Enid noticed first. She looked like she'd just seen a very clever magic trick and she couldn't figure out how it was done. She was just kind of . . . staring.

Then Epiphany noticed Enid noticing, so she noticed next. Then finally, Abby looked over and saw Tyler – her ex-boyfriend – with his arm around me – her ex-best-friend . . .

And she smiled.

Zach was busy tying and untying her shoelaces affectionately.

Enid and Epiphany eventually recovered from the shock of seeing Melody Moss with a boyfriend.

Victor swapped his ham sandwich with my goat's-cheese-and-raisin couscous.

And the whole time, Tyler had his arm around me.

As if it was just a normal Monday.

# CHAPTER 40: Happy Fools

Tuesday, 10 June

5.06pm

Day 3

of having a boyfriend ☺.

At Broadway Babies today, we watched the movie of *Wicked* in preparation for our visit to the theatre next Saturday. Miss Elliot made microwave popcorn, and we all sang along like happy fools, until Maud got the hiccups, which can happen if you snack and sing. We tried all the usual methods to cure her:

- We got her to drink water upside down: she got very wet and it didn't work.
- We all joined hands in a circle and held our breath with her: she got dizzy and it didn't work.
- I screamed at her unexpectedly to give her a fright: she burst into tears, and it worked.

Afterwards, I asked Miss Elliot if Tyler could come on our excursion to see the show, even though he's not in Broadway Babies. She said yes, he could be an honorary member for the day because he was in our musical last term.

As if that day couldn't get more exciting!

# CHAPTER 41: Score!

Thursday, 12 June
7.00pm

Day 5

of having a boyfriend ☺.

Tyler wanted to watch me play basketball after school. I was so excited-slash-embarrassed because I'm still not very good, but I guess having someone watching, just for me, gave me confidence and I even scored a basket!

After the game, Connor asked Tyler if he wanted to join the club, and Tyler said yes! So, next term Tyler and I will be doing basketball together. Woo-hoo!!!!

**Exploring new interests this term: tick.** ☑

Two

days

till

*Wicked*!!

# CHAPTER 42: Last Day

Friday, 13 June
5.30pm

Day 6 ♡

of having a boyfriend ☺.

Today was our last day of term and Victor's last day at our school. Thankfully, we have *Wicked* tomorrow to take the edge off the sadness.

Mum made cupcakes for me to take in. Each one had a letter from Victor's name on top. We had a little party in our spot at lunch and had fun rearranging the cupcakes to spell different things.

Then we threw them out because they were green and tasted like those pine-tree air fresheners that taxi drivers use.

After school, Victor and Tyler came back to my house for pizza and a movie. None of us could decide what to watch, though, so we ended up scrolling through funny animal videos on YouTube, which made Toto very barky and farty, which made pizza-eating a challenge, but we managed.

Six months ago, I never would have imagined being so happy in the company of two actual boys, but here we are.

# CHAPTER 43: Starstruck

Saturday, 14 June
8.30am

One week

of having a boyfriend ☺.

## It's *Wicked* day!!!

Tyler is coming over at midday and Mum's going to drop us into town to meet the others for the show, which starts at 2pm.

I have absolutely **zero chill**.

5.30pm

When Tyler arrived, he gave me an Elphaba squishy toy!

'Happy one-week anniversary,' he said.

'Oh, is it?' I said, as though I didn't know. 'Thank you! I love it! Happy anniversary.'

He kissed me on the cheek in that sweet way he has done exactly twelve times now, not that I'm counting, and gave me a hug.

Tyler hugs are like:

- Falling into a very soft bed made of clouds.
- Swimming in a warm, blue ocean.
- Lying on the grass on a summer's day.
- Eating mango-flavoured gelato.

When Mum drove us into town. I insisted on playing the *Wicked* soundtrack all the way there, because I was **beside myself**. Tyler was also beside me because we were sitting in the back seat while Mum was totes our Uber driver. She didn't mind though, she's very happy that I have my first boyfriend.

We met Miss Elliot, Victor, Abby, Zach, Enid, Epiphany, Simone, Maud and the others out the front of the theatre. Abby and Zach were both dressed in all green LOL.

We sat excitedly in the theatre, amazed by the huge moving dragon on the set.

As soon as the orchestra played the first few notes I spontaneously burst into tears. I couldn't believe I was about to watch my favourite show ever for the very first time.

The show was **INCREDIBLE**. Tyler held my hand the whole time and laughed at me every time I cried, **which was a lot**.

Afterwards, Miss Elliot took us to the Stage Door.

A stage manager all in black, with a headset, came to meet us. She looked at Simone and said, 'I like your backpack.' It was the first time I've ever seen Simone speechless.

The stage manager then took us **onto the actual stage** of *Wicked*, where we had just seen all these incredible performers singing and acting their heads off. It was amazing to look out at the hundreds of seats in the audience.

Soon, five of the cast members from the show, who knew Miss Elliot, came out onto the stage.

'Thanks for doing this between shows,' Miss Elliot said to the actress playing Glinda and **HUGGED HER.**

I couldn't believe they had to do the whole show again in just a couple of hours! How do they do it? I don't think I could ever be a performer.

Abby was very emotional. 'I feel like this is where I am meant to be,' she said, fanning her face dramatically.

Victor rolled his eyes at me, and I stifled a laugh.

The actress playing Glinda was **so nice** to us. She even let us take a photo, which is now my screensaver on my computer and my phone, and I will probably get a full body tattoo of it.

In it are the five *Wicked* cast members, Miss Elliot, me, my (ahem) boyfriend Tyler, Victor and all our gang, standing on the on the set of *Wicked*.

<u>Life</u>

<u>Made</u>.

<u>5.35pm</u>

*Hang on a minute . . .*

I was just looking at the photo again and there's someone in it that I'm sure wasn't there on the day. Right on the end, dressed in rags, looking like a character from the show, but not.

*Who is that person?*

Then it hit me.

The *M*ysterious Stranger! With her arm around me! Smiling mysteriously!

***What the . . .*** ???

I think I've officially lost the plot.

Thank the Sweet Baby Cheeses it's the school holidays!

# About the Author

**Helen Dallimore** is an actress, singer, director and writer who lives in Sydney's inner west with her husband, son and West Highland White Terrier called Gnocchi.

She graduated from NIDA sometime last century, and somehow ended up in London's West End starring as the original Glinda in *Wicked* opposite Idina Menzel – whaaaat?

She's been in a bunch of telly, movies, plays and musicals, usually as the comic relief. Her dedication to making people laugh led her to start writing for TV comedies including ABC's *Sando* and Channel 9's *Here Come the Habibs*, in which she also starred.

Helen likes chocolate, cheese, dogs, swimming in the sea and laughing till she wees. She does not like queuing, bad food or being cold. She hopes you enjoy this, her second novel, and that it makes you wee.